Kate did not sleep, or lose consciousness completely, but lapsed into a queer, semi-waking state. Her eyes, half-open, ached in the sunlight reflected from one dingy wall. But she did not even blink, afraid that if she tried to move she would find that she could not.

There were feet on the stairs, voices outside the door, then in the room with her. Three or four men, talking in low voices. A couple of them wore fur-collared blue Chicago police winter jackets, with badges on their fur-flapped caps. She could see details very clearly whenever they came into the center of her field of vision.

They'll take me home, Kate thought, they'll snap me out of this. One of the men took her arm to lift it. It clung to her side, amazingly stiff, resisting her pull without the least effort on her part.

The policeman said, "My guess is two, three days since she died."

AN OLD FRIEND OF THE FAMILY

AN OLD FRIEND OF THE FAMILY

FRED SABERHAGEN

A TOM DOHERTY ASSOCIATES BOOK

AN OLD FRIEND OF THE FAMILY

Reprinted by arrangement with the author

First Tor printing: March 1987

A TOR Book

Published by Tom Doherty Associates, Inc.
49 West 24 Street
New York, N.Y. 10010

Cover art by Joe DeVito

ISBN: 0-812-52550-7
CAN. ED.: 0-812-52551-5

Printed in the United States of America

0 9 8 7 6 5 4 3 2

One

It looked like the North Atlantic raging at the Devon coast, Kate told herself, recalling a childhood trip to Europe, and the enduring memory of the ocean pounding at those rough English rocks. Now, under the glare of the close-ranked floodlights along the Outer Drive, she saw the black lake reach a fist in past the wintry void, where summer knew a strip of sunwhite beach. Above the ice-draped slats of snowfence the fist shook spume at city and civilization, then crashed down, dissolving itself in an open-handed splash that washed across six of the eight lanes of forty-mile-per-hour traffic. The traffic wavered, minimally slowing, some of it skidding perilously in the freezing wet. If things kept on this way, the police were going to have to close the Drive.

Twenty or thirty yards inland, on pavement separated from the Drive and the reaching waves

1

by a wide divider strip of frozen parkland, Kate's
Lancia purred sedately south. Most of her attention was concentrated upon the task of reading
addresses from the endless row of tall apartment
buildings fronting on Drive and park and lake.
The particular numbers she had been looking for
now suddenly appeared, elegantly backlighted
against a towering granite wall. She slowed and
turned. The righthand curve of driveway went
down to a basement garage, but she stayed with
the left branch, rolled past two parked Cadillacs
and a Porsche, and pulled up under the building's
entrance canopy.

Despite the heatlamps fighting down against
the wind and cold, the uniformed doorman wore
earmuffs above the collar of his winter jacket. His
eyeglasses were so thick as to resemble frosted
protective goggles of some sort. Taller than he,
Kate swept in through the door that he held open
for her, meanwhile pulling back the hood of her
warm blue jacket from natural blond curls.

"I'd like to see Craig Walworth. Tell him Kate
Southerland is here," she told the man when he
had followed her into the lobby. A few moments
later, after the intercom had brought down Craig's
acceptance of her visit, she was alone in a small
elevator.

If Joe were with her now, he'd be worrying
about what the doorman was going to do with the
car—or about something else, about anything,
maybe just about dropping in on a party unan-
nounced. But then if Joe were with her tonight,
she wouldn't be coming here at all. Which, of
course, was really the whole point. She hadn't

made any commitment to Joe—not yet. If and when she did, things would be different.

And how they would.

Maybe the real point was the fact that she felt compelled to make the point. If she was so certain of her present freedom, why was she here trying to prove something to herself? She could have gone Christmas shopping instead. And she probably should have. For one thing she still faced the problem of a gift for Joe, who was certain to spend too much of his money buying one for her . . .

The elevator, having gone as high as it could go, eased almost imperceptibly to a stop and let Kate out into a small marble lobby from which two massive doors of handcarved black wood, one at each end, led to two apartments. A small decorative table, ivory-colored to contrast with the doors, stood in the middle of the lobby facing the two elevators. On the wall just above the table there hung a picture, or perhaps it was a mirror, of which only an edge of antique gilt frame was visible. Someone had draped an old, worn-looking raincoat over it, perhaps thinking that the loser of the garment would be sure to see it there if he came back. He'd need something warmer than that if he came back tonight.

The right hand door stood slightly ajar, and through this opening came sounds of subdued partying: music, an alto laugh, a glassy clink, and voices murmuring. Kate pushed the thick door fully open and slowly walked on in. She stood in a brick-floored vestibule, from which two interior hallways led off at right angles to each other. A third wall was taken up by a great guest closet, open now to show a modest miscellany of coats and scarves, some fallen from their hangers. It didn't seem that any very large party was going on.

"Hi." The greeting was conspiratorially low. Simultaneously a black-haired, black-bearded head bobbed into Kate's view from two rooms down the hallway to her right. Craig Walworth was three or four years older than her twenty. No more than an inch taller, but so wide across the chest that he looked larger than he was. Often, as now, his shirt was worn halfway open down the front to display some hair and muscle; and he tended to have his large hands planted on his hips—one of them was there now, the other holding a drink—so that standing near him put you at some risk from jutting elbows. "Glad you could make it, Kate. I was starting to think you were really out of circulation." The drink he had been holding somehow already stashed away, he took her jacket as she slipped it off, and with a toss consigned it to the closet's minor chaos.

"You put out a standing invitation for Friday nights, Craig. I'm just taking you at your word."

"I'm just delighted that you are, Sweetie. Our little group here will never be the same—thank God." Craig's voice was still low, uncharacteristically near the whispering level, and now he glanced about, a man checking to see if he might be overheard. "Now listen, Doll, there's a little house rule I've got to mention before you join the group."

"Rules? That's not quite what I would have expected at your parties."

"Well, you see, it's not your basic expectable

kind of rule." As they talked, he had started her moving down the hall toward the still rather muffled sounds of partying, with an arm round her waist that she somehow minded more than the expected cheek-kiss following. "The thing is, everyone—except me, of course—takes a new name for the evening, and pretends to be someone other than they are. You should be . . . how do you like Sabrina? Sabrina Something, and I'll say that you're an old friend of mine from Canada. How's that?"

"Well, I did think of becoming Sabrina once, believe it or not. When I was about thirteen years old."

They had now come to a room where four or five people were gathered, all standing, as if none of them had been here very long. Kate so rarely remembered names the first time round that sometimes she was tempted to give up trying; and since these were supposedly all aliases anyway, she made no effort to retain anything from the round of introductions.

Beside Kate stood a tall girl wearing an odd shawl who wanted to find out how much Kate knew about Tarot cards. When she heard the answer was nothing at all, she wanted to explain them at great length. Kate tried for a little while to make sense of it, and then, as the group shifted, took the first opportunity to move away. She was offered a drink, declined, then thought that the next time she would accept. In the background she could hear a heavy door, probably the front door of the apartment, being firmly closed. Craig had excused himself, and was somewhere around a corner, talking on the phone.

"Try a joint?" This from a stocky young man with thick glasses who had not been in the group the first time round—no doubt there might be other people she had not met, in other rooms; it must be a huge apartment. The man making the offer got too close, and stared at Kate intensely. Being given a man's full attention is a thrilling experience for a woman—well, sometimes. Hadn't she seen him somewhere else recently? But she had no intention of asking that aloud.

Kate puffed twice and put the thing down. As expected, she felt nothing from it just at first. The first few times that she had tried, in school, nothing at all had happened to her. The few times after that had always resulted in a pleasant high, with slow onset and letdown. She wouldn't be surprised if it was nothing at all again tonight; quite likely she was just too keyed up, too nervous, though why she should be . . .

" . . . play games in a little while, you know, identities and such." Craig was back at her side, finishing a statement whose beginning Kate had somehow missed. "And someone else is coming, Sabrina, someone I want you to meet. I've mentioned you to him, and he's very interested."

"Oh? My Canadian background?"

Craig's eyes were sparkling with some inner amusement under their dark brows. But now his attention was forced away by someone else, a blondish boy with a loud mouth, who had some interminable anecdote to tell him, as one insider to another. Craig responded with off-hand but deliberate insults, which the loud one laughed at foolishly.

Kate almost tripped over the tall girl, then sat down beside her on the thick, burgundy-colored carpet. "What sort of games is he talking about?" Kate asked. The girl said something Kate couldn't catch. Very loud music was starting in the next room. The Pointer Sisters?

Upon the wall that Kate was facing there hung an Escher print, the circle of lizards crawling up out of the flat surface of the drawing-within-the-drawing, crawling up and around an improvised ramp of books and geometric solids, to ease themselves at last down into the flat again, where in three shades of gray their bodies formed a tessellated pattern. Kate willed for a moment to lose herself in the intricacies of the plan, but her mind was too restless.

She looked around abruptly, with the feeling that someone, no one she knew, had just called her real name: a loud, rude calling in a strange man's voice. But no one else seemed to have noticed it at all. And the voice seemed to have come, now that she thought about it, directly into her mind, not through her ears. Dear Kate, she warned herself, neither you nor Sabrina had better smoke any more tonight.

Restlessness pulled her to her feet. A bar-on-a-cart offered bottles and glasses and ice. Shouldn't mix with the other stuff, but just a taste was not going to do her any harm. In her hand a glass half-filled with white wine, she wandered, mocking a slinky tall-model walk, up to a window of very solid, unopenable glass that looked out far above the endless chains of headlights and taillights of the Drive. Beyond the few additional streetlamps that were scattered through the park, the lake stretched out to the edge of everything, a vast black invisibility like death.

One of the nameless boys she had just met came to the window too, ice cubes tinkling in his glass like Christmas music. God, the shopping she had yet to do. What was she here for, anyway? Trying to prove a point to Joe, who didn't know where she was, and who, when she told him, would fail to get the—

Her name again, but still unspoken.

Looking down a vista of the apartment's archways, Kate saw a huge, dark-haired man standing gazing toward her. An early Orson Welles, but harder-faced, in a brown coat made of one of those rich fake-furs, like her own blue. Or maybe in his case the fur was real. He was standing there as if he had just arrived, though if her sense of the place was right, he was nowhere near the front entrance.

With a vague feeling that it was important, necessary for her to do so, Kate turned from the window and walked toward the newcomer. No one else seemed to be paying either of them the least attention. The Pointer Sisters grew louder still, then faded abruptly as a door somewhere behind Kate was closed. She was alone with the huge man in the hallway—no, not quite alone. From the corner of her eye Kate saw Craig walk out of another doorway to her left. Craig fell into step beside her as she walked the last few strides toward the big man who stood waiting.

They stopped. Craig put his hands on his hips, then at once let them slide off to hang fidgeting at his sides. "Enoch Winter," he said, almost whispering again, "this is Kathryn Southerland."

The huge man said something (what?) to her in an offhand sort of greeting, and she replied. He was really massive, and Kate was reminded of when she had met an All-American defensive end: perfect proportions, but blown up larger than real life seemed to have the right to be.

Enoch Winter's dark hair was slightly curly, and worn shorter than that of most young men. There were only the beginnings of lines in his face. Still, at second glance Kate would not have called him young if she had had to set down a description. His eyes were gray-blue, his broad, pale cheeks a little blue with what would be heavy stubble in a few hours if he let it grow. He was smiling confidently at Kate, and all but ignoring Craig. He spoke to her again; once more she somehow could not grasp what he had said.

There was a brief distraction as the short young man with thick eyeglasses appeared from somewhere to stand at Kate's right, looking on in silence. The four of them in the hallway were closed off now by doors on every side. Beyond the closed doors, the sounds of the party went on.

Enoch Winter spoke, and Kate stared at him, straining to understand. His voice was loud enough. And she had thought the pot would not take hold of her tonight. She shouldn't even have tasted the wine.

He chuckled, perhaps at something he had just said himself. He didn't seem to notice that she could not comprehend what he was saying. Or else he did not care. With a faint inward start Kate realized that Craig and Thick-glasses were no longer at her sides. They had gone away somewhere, leaving her standing in the shut-off hall with Enoch Winter, who talked and talked, to her alone. She must not ever let her attention waver from him for a moment, must not . . .

His whitish hand, raised, was so big that the great dark stone that rode one finger in a silver ring seemed not only modest but scarcely adequate. Just past his waving hand Kate's eye caught sight of a phone on a hall table, and it came to her with desperate force that there was something she must do at once.

"Excuse me a moment," she broke in clearly. "I've got to call home right away."

" . . . hafta do that for?" His accent was midwestern, vaguely rural. All of a sudden he wasn't happy any more.

"I have to. That's all." Walking to the phone was the most utterly wearying thing that Kate had ever done. She managed to do it, though.

" . . . careful whatcha say. All right." Enoch's voice had regained some of its good humor, and now good-humoredly he fell silent.

Kate punched at buttons. She could hear the phone at home start ringing, and then a familiar voice.

"Hello, Gran. I just wanted to tell you . . . " What could she say? What was she able to say? "I didn't do any shopping after all. So I couldn't get those things you wanted."

"Well, goodness, dear. Don't worry about it. You sound upset, are you all right?"

"Fine."

"Well, I expect I'll be going out myself tomorrow, I can do my own shopping. Where are you?"

A leaden pause, in which Kate could feel her own mind groping. Crawling. Trying to get free, but leashed. "Downtown," she got out at last. It was almost the truth, the closest thing to truth that she could manage.

"Take care now, Kate, they say the roads are very nasty."

As she cradled the phone Enoch started talking to her again. In this case it really was flattering to have such concentrated attention from a man, attention of a kind she could not get often enough from Joe.

Somehow or other they now were standing by the guest closet and Enoch was watching while she put on her blue jacket. In some far-off room of the apartment voices were cheering now— probably a game was being played. Craig was here again, though, to see them out in silence. Enoch tossed a—condescending?—wink at Craig, whose own face displayed a vast . . . well, admiration, as though for something Enoch was doing or had done. Kate puzzled over all this while she walked out to the elevator, her hand on Enoch's arm.

Going down with Enoch, she thought for the most part about nothing at all. While he perhaps was thinking of her, for once or twice he put out his huge, pale hand and brushed her cheek with it, rather as if she were something that he had long coveted and had just allowed himself to buy. She wouldn't like it if Joe behaved so possessively. But this was different . . . of course.

The elevator let them out in the subterranean

garage, and there was her Lancia, keys and all.
Kate slipped into the driver's seat, Enoch waiting
till he was invited to get in on the right. There was
no doorman to be seen, but gates opened ahead of
them and out they went, into the cold and up the
curving driveway.

Kate drove, without having to think of where to
go. As before, Enoch talked, and it seemed to her
that she could not understand a word. White needles filled bright globes of air around the streetlights. In some clear corner of Kate's mind the
thought occurred that nothing she had ever
smoked before had hit her this way. Once the
situation struck her as so ridiculous that she
began to laugh, and laughed so hard and so wildly
that it was difficult for her to see where she was
steering. Enoch spoke sharply to her and she
calmed down. Then it was his turn to laugh,
loudly and heartily, evidently at something Kate
had just tried to say. The trouble was that something in his laughter hurt Kate's ears, so she
wanted to put her fingers into them, but instead
she had to go on driving.

They had already turned inland, away from the
lake, leaving the Outer Drive and the Gold Coast
behind. Was this Diversey she was following
now? She wasn't sure. Probably they were farther
south. Presently she turned again, going where
she had to go. Here the street lamps were fewer,
and gave a different light, wan and wintry. It was
surprising how in the city the neighborhoods
could change from one block to the next.

Now here was where they were to stop. Certainly no doorman here, in fact not even a break in
the row of dull vehicles parked along the frozen

curb. Near the end of the block a fireplug-space at least was open, and Kate halted just ahead of it and started to back in.

A car just behind them turned into the same space headfirst, jounced to a halt there just as Kate also hit her brakes. At the moment both vehicles had a tirehold on the precious space, but neither could occupy it.

She turned to Enoch helplessly. There was an abstracted expression on his face; he opened his door and got out. His head vanished from Kate's view, but from the attitude of his body it was plain that he was facing back into the glare of their challenger's headlights. Cold air swirled in through the open door to paw Kate's legs. An engine gunned behind them; the other car was backing away. Enoch slid in beside her again and closed the door, the look on his face unchanged.

Kate parked the car—must have parked it, though the next thing she was aware of was walking along the cracked and narrow sidewalk beside Enoch, whose arm encircled her but brought no warmth. The footing was treacherous, half uneven pavement, half blackened ice in old refrozen mounds, all under a powdering of new snow. When had she ever felt cold so intense before?

They passed beneath an ancient neon sign humming to itself and sizzling with unplanned flashes. A man went by them, his face as hard and his clothes as grimy as the street itself. Suddenly there were two wooden steps, a narrow door that yielded to Enoch's shoulder, and now at least the wind was gone.

The cold kept pace, though, as they walked up stairs, bare wood creaking underfoot beneath the gritty crunching of a layer of grime. It would be terrible to have to face a night like this alone, but she would not, no, she would not. She clung hard now to Enoch's arm.

He used a key, then brought her through a door into a room of utter cold, a wretchedly furnished room, dark but for pale streetlight coming in through an undraped window. Kate saw smeared glass, one broken pane with rags stuffed into it.

"You'll have to hold me," she whispered, shivering violently. "I'm here and I can't help myself, you know. At least hold me so I won't be so cold."

He laughed. When he spoke now she could hear him plainly. "Oh, I'll hold you, okay. You'll get to like it here. Think of it as home, maybe, even. Wise little rich-bitch." He had closed the door and was standing right in front of her. "You think you know just what is gonna happen now. But you don't know at all, at all."

Then he seemed to descend upon her like a great slow wave from the black lake.

Two

In the rather more than thirty years since Clarissa Southerland had come to live in Glenlake, this was almost the first time that anyone on the village police force had spoken to her in line of duty. And it occurred to her to wonder now, somewhat belatedly no doubt, whether this aloofness from the cops was after all not a continent-wide American peculiarity, but simply the result of living in a wealthy suburb. In England as a girl and young woman she had chatted with the constables routinely; but England, of course, was different.

Detective Franzen, a balding, sad-looking young man, was listening to Clarissa's account of Kate's last phone call home with every appearance of totally absorbed, sympathetic attention. His behavior was not at all like that of the New York detectives, years ago, that time the jewels were taken at the hotel. Meanwhile Kate's mother,

Lenore, was standing behind Franzen and wor-
riedly eyeing her mother-in-law as if Clarissa
were some undependable child who might not
perform creditably for the nice policeman. Behind Lenore was the closed door to the study, and
behind *that* in turn was Andrew, busy talking on
the phone to his office, where people were sure to
be working even on Saturday, working on something vital that demanded some of Andrew's attention, even on the day of a missing daughter.

"Now, Mrs. Southerland, do you remember
there being any unusual background noises on
the phone? Sometimes there's a typewriter,
or . . ."

"Not at parties, there isn't very often." Suddenly Clarissa began to lose confidence in Franzen, nice manners or not. It made her feel fidgety,
and she wished she had taken a rocking chair,
instead of this plush one, which was too soft.

"Oh, you did hear partying noises then?"

"Yes, I believe I mentioned that before." Hadn't
she? She couldn't confirm from Lenore's or Franzen's expressions now whether she had or not.
"People laughing, way in the background. Ice,
tinkling in a glass? No, I couldn't swear to that."

"And all she said about her location was that
she was downtown?"

"Yes."

"Anyone call anyone by name?"

Clarissa took thought. Sometimes one gained
impressions of things not exactly by hearing
them, and later it was hard to sort out what one
had actually heard and what one had not. "Not
that I recall."

Franzen, poker-faced, seated on a straight chair

opposite, studied his notebook. "Well. You all tell me that this staying out all night without letting someone know is not something that Kate's ever done—"

"It certainly isn't," put in Lenore.

"—and here it is well after noon. So, I think we'd better take it seriously enough to check it out. The Chicago police, and so on." Franzen stood up, just as the door to the study opened. Andrew, balding too, but athletic and agressive in his mid-forties, came out to join the conversation.

"What progress have we made?" Andrew demanded with brisk intensity. Here was a man switching his attention from one crisis to another, and someone had better have ready a satisfactory, concise briefing for him if they wanted his advice and help on the problem of locating his daughter, because some new emergency regarding business was surely going to come up soon and keep him from spending a lot of time on this one.

This, at least, was the impression his mother got of him at the moment. Clarissa, feeling a twinge of guilt because there were times when she just didn't like her own son very much, grunted and hand-fought her way up out of the too-soft chair: the knees and hips were not too good today. Muttering a few words of farewell to Detective Franzen, she left the search for her granddaughter in the hands of those who were now in charge of running the world, and took herself off to the library, meaning to have a look at the lake through her favorite window.

In the room lined with shelves of dark wood, with the door closed behind her, it was quiet, the murmur of concerned voices almost left behind.

Beyond the double Thermopane a field of virgin snow, fallen mostly in the dark hours of the morning, sloped away to disappear over the top of a thirty-foot bluff some forty yards behind the house. Looking past that brink, Clarissa could see a mile or more south along the gently curving shoreline of Lake Michigan. There were trees, there were the houses of the wealthy. The beach was completely hidden beneath a frigid wilderness of ice-cakes, foot-thick slabs that had been broken by waves, washed in and upended in a crazy jumble, stretching for lifeless kilometers under the lifeless sun of afternoon. Beyond the icefields, dark open water reached victorious, almost calm now, to the horizon.

A voice asked: "Granny?"

In jeans and old shirt Judy leaned against the jamb of the re-opened library door. Three years younger than the missing Kate, somewhat darker of hair and eye, more strongly built, not quite as conventionally pretty—but quite possibly, their grandmother thought, fated to be the more beautiful of the two when both were full-grown women.

Smiling involuntarily, Clarissa turned from the window. "What is it, dear?"

The girl was solemn. "Is there any news yet?"

"No. Except it seems that the police are going to start looking for her."

"Has anyone called Joe?"

"I doubt that anyone has. And I think you're right; it's probably time that someone did."

Judy's eyes, as they often did, seemed to be probing for the true thoughts of the person she was speaking to. "Do you want to, Gran? Or I will if you like."

Clarissa hesitated, then answered with a nod. Calling Joe was best not left to Andrew or Lenore. "You have the touch, Judy. He'll take bad news—or alarming news anyway—better coming from you than anyone else. If you don't mind." Helping was what this girl had to do when she was worried, as some people had to mope and others to cry. Blessed is the family, Clarissa thought, that has a Judy in it; and I don't know of any other one than ours.

Judy was gone, considerately closing the door behind her. But Clarissa had hardly turned toward the icefields again when it opened again. "Hey, Gran?" a deeper voice inquired.

This was Johnny, the baby of the house. At sixteen he was a strong-jawed, slightly shorter version of his father, one notable difference being Johnny's teen-length, light brown curls. "They're all still busy in there, Gran. If anyone's looking for me, I'm going over to Clark's. He's got that new computer kit."

"Don't be late, Johnny. I'm sure your mother will want you back before dark today."

"Aw, Gran, c'mon. Kate's all right." No doubts at all were going to be tolerated on that point. "She's a big girl. I mean, I know my sister can take care of herself out there."

"And you're grown up too, or very nearly. Yes. But don't be late?"

She made it a question rather than a hopeless attempt at an order, and Johnny at least smiled and waved before he left, so maybe he would at least consider what his grandmother had said. Then he was gone, and there was no longer anything to interfere with Clarissa's looking out the window. It took her only a minute to discover that that was not what she wanted to do after all.

It was good to get away from the tension in the family for a little while, to have time for her own thoughts. But why had she chosen the library? Had it been in the back of her mind to find something particular to read?

Clarissa was staring up at the east end of the highest shelf on the south wall when with a minor inward shock she consciously remembered what was up there. Years, it had been, since she had even thought of that. She shook her head deliberately, and deliberately smiled at herself, and moved away. But her steps slowed as she neared the door, which Johnny had left open. Clarissa closed it slowly. She did not want to rejoin the others just yet, she wanted to stay here.

She had been seated in an armchair for ten minutes, reading lamp on beside her, reading a John O'Hara novel, when she suddenly fully understood that she had stationed herself here on guard, on call. She was on sentry duty, a few paces from the east end of the high south shelves. This time she did not try to smile at all.

Three

On regaining consciousness, Kate was no longer bothered by the cold, and at first she knew a trace of fear that hers were the sensations of death-by-freezing. But her fingers and toes were perfectly flexible and sensitive, her ears were not at all numb, and she was not shivering. Still cold in the room, certainly, but her body was coping with it now. A sort of second wind, evidently—or a second warmth might be a better way to put it.

It was still night, though now she could see the room and its poor furnishings much more clearly than before. Maybe another electric sign had been turned on outside, or more likely her eyes had simply adjusted to the dark. She thought that not much time had passed, for she seemed still to be feeling the effects of what she had smoked, combined with the white wine. But now she was completely alone.

She could remember Enoch's face above hers in

the dark, and his weight, pressing her down on the poor bed, where she still lay on her back, atop whatever bedclothes there might be. A forced intimacy, certainly, but not, as far as she could tell, a conventional rape. She was still fully dressed, lying there with her right arm thrown back above her head, and her left hand resting loosely on her middle.

Kate sat up, easily, not hurting anywhere, groping with her toes automatically for one shoe that had fallen off. With this strange high of hers she was not in the mood to wonder about the why of anything, to worry about whether she had actually been raped or not.

Both shoes on, Kate stood up, a little giddily just at first, and observed that she was still wearing her warm blue jacket. There appeared to be nothing to do in this room, so at once she headed for the door.

She went quickly down the creaky stairs, and out into the shabby, unfamiliar street. At the moment fear and worry were as remote to her as curiosity. Maybe in the morning she would have the world's worst hangover, but right now she simply felt like walking. The sky had cleared, as clear as it ever got above the city itself.

Still feeling immune to cold and wind, Kate set out, marching in a direction she was sure was east, and noting the steady diminution of the address numbers that she passed, numbers that seemed to indicate that she had not too far to go, to reach the shops on North Michigan. These days all the best shopping was up there, not in the Loop.

She passed a man who turned to look at her, perhaps only wondering that she dared to walk Chicago's streets at night and alone. In this neighborhood there were only a few people about. What time was it, anyway? Might the stores be closed? Kate's watch showed 7:48 when she pressed its button—which was odd, considering that it must have been later than that when she left Craig's. But she was not capable of trying to puzzle it all out now. She was going to walk.

She came upon Michigan Boulevard from the west, passing through a region of closed printing shops, closed antique dealers, nearly empty parking lots, ad agencies all but anonymous behind their discreet signs, walls, and shutters. An elegant restaurant was open, so was a fast-food place a block away. She didn't feel at all hungry. Here was a subway entrance. She had ridden the subway and El once with Johnny, from Evanston all the way down through the city to the far South Side and back again, just to see what it was like, and nothing had happened to them at all, though their parents had been angry when they found out . . . and here were the stairs to the upper level of Michigan, where she would find the shops she wanted.

And here on the upper level were the shops at last, open till all hours of the night on these last shopping days before Christmas; here were the well-dressed crowds struggling muffled through the decorated streets against a wind that did not bother Kate. The traffic inched. The buses roared, befouled the air, crept ahead two, three, four of them together sometimes, threatening to crush their way right through the endless herds of walking bodies that bravely disputed every crosswalk with the vehicles.

Kate was on the point of entering a store before she realized that she had with her no money and no credit cards. She couldn't remember now whether or not she had been carrying a handbag when she went up to Craig's. She must have been carrying money and cards for shopping. And so somehow they must have been left at Craig's, or in that strange little room.

She wondered, without any real concern one way or the other, if Enoch might have taken them, and if Enoch had returned to the ugly little room by now. She wondered also, every now and then, if she were dreaming, because this high of hers seemed to be just going on and on; there had to be something more than pot, or even pot and wine, involved in it. If she went back to her car, and it hadn't been stolen or stripped or towed away, she might drive home . . . but first she wanted to do some shopping. With this in mind she walked into a store, and then remembered that she had no money . . .

Around and around went the cycle, like a fever-dream. At one point it stuttered and broke, and she found herself in a phone booth, using small change discovered in her jacket pocket, punching numbers. Joe's voice on the line, saying *hello*, came like a tonic shock, a shock that if it went on very long might threaten to wake her up, and in a moment she had hung up the receiver without speaking. He must never see her like this, he must never know . . . but now she had to find a gift for Joe. She had known him now for more than a year, and had never given him a thing that really mattered . . .

The crowd of shoppers had thinned to a mere scattering of people, the stores on the verge of closing, before the cycle broke finally and she was free. Or was she? First, back to the room, of course. Her valuables must be there, and her car was parked nearby. For some reason her life, her new life, centered there now. *You'll get to like it here. Think of it as home, maybe even.*

Kate did not feel physically tired, and walked back at a brisk pace. Approaching the dingy building, she looked for the Lancia, but the space by the hydrant was empty now. Still, she felt no alarm at the discovery.

Walking up the gritty stairs she met no one, though now a radio was playing somewhere in the building, making it seem not entirely deserted. Now what? She had been through all her pockets several times, and was certain that she didn't have a key. She pressed her body against the room's door, though, and it quite smoothly let her in.

Kate made sure that the door was locked behind her. Then, feeling a little dizzy though not exactly tired, she threw herself down on the bed. Her right arm fell back over her head. One of her shoes fell off.

She did not sleep, or lose consciousness completely, but lapsed into a queer, semi-waking state, during which she was aware of the gradual brightening of the room into full daylight. Kate's eyes, half-open, ached in the sunlight reflected from one dingy wall. But she did not even blink, being afraid that if she tried to move she would find that she could not.

There were feet on the stairs, several heavy people coming up. Voices outside the door, then in the room with her. Three or four men in the room, standing about, talking in low voices. A couple of them wore fur-collared blue Chicago police winter jackets, with badges on their fur-flapped caps. She could see details very plainly whenever they came into the center of her field of vision.

They'll take me home, Kate thought, they'll snap me out of this. Not that she cared, yet, whether they did or not. But gathering in the back of her mind was the first inkling of concern, taking form like the knowledge that the dentist's numbing shot is presently going to wear off.

Starting to grow curious at last, she harkened to what the men were saying.

" . . . so cold, it could be hard to tell."

"Yeah."

One took her arm to lift it. It clung to her side, amazingly stiff, resisting his pull without the least effort on her part.

He said, "My own guess is two, three days since she died."

Four

Clarissa was sitting in the breakfast room, the cup of coffee that Judy had insisted on pouring for her still untouched, when the sound of wheels on the drive announced the return of Andrew and Lenore from the Chicago morgue.

Judy jumped up and hurried on ahead, and was almost in the front hall before the old woman could start moving. By the time Clarissa reached the entry, Lenore was inside the house, winter coat still on, sobbing in her younger daughter's arms as if they were her mother's. Andrew came in much more slowly, forgetting at first to shut the outer door behind him. His cheeks were for once unshaven, displaying sandy stubble, and loose flesh showed at his collar where it seemed that yesterday there had been none. His coat still on too, buttoned and forgotten, he leaned against the wall and muttered as if to himself.

"They're going to do an autopsy on Monday. I

asked, why not tomorrow? They said some tox-
icologist is coming in Sunday night, it would be
better if they wait for him.''

The last word dissolved into a grating sob. Judy
got an arm free from her mother, and pulled her
father's head down on her shoulder to give comfort.

Sometime much later in that dazed day, Andrew became aware that Joe Keogh was in the
house, wandering about, looking as bewildered
and grief-stricken as anyone else. Poor Irish
roughneck cop who had thought he was going to
marry into wealth. Never have to face the prospect of him as a son-in-law now. Never have to.
Never . . .

So peaceful Kate had been there on the antisep-
tic public table. He tried to hold in mind that
peaceful, contented look, more like one sleeping
than one dead. That look would seem to show she
had not suffered. Dying there in that sleazy rooming house. What was she doing there? With
whom? Someone must have been there. But Andrew was not ready to face those questions just
yet.

So considerate were all of the officials, holding
down the publicity as well and as long as they
could. Though in the long run they wouldn't be
able to, he understood that. He couldn't estimate
yet the effect on business, good or bad. Just one of
those things that could not be planned for . . .
time enough for that tomorrow.

. . . Judy of course went to place herself by the
young man when he sat down, and held his
prizefighter's hand. That was her way.

Meanwhile more police—Andrew lost track of what separate organizations they all represented—were in the house and out again. They talked to Andrew, and ten minutes later he couldn't remember what they had asked or he had answered. You planned and worked, and built up your business, all for your family, and then . . .

Johnny, as red-eyed as the rest of the family and for once subdued, came along in late afternoon with the word that he was going over to Clark's for a while, if his parents didn't mind. The Birches were close friends and it was natural that they would want to share the burden of the tragedy.

Andrew spoke to his son in a painful voice. "I don't think you're in shape right now to be driving." He could not really remember himself driving home from Chicago. "I don't think any of us are."

"I'll walk, Dad." The Birches lived only about two hundred yards away along Sheridan Road, where the shoulders, though unpaved, were smooth and plenty wide enough to walk on without having to dodge traffic.

"All right, then. Tell them we'll call them later."

Shortly after Johnny left, darkness fell.

The phone rang, rang. Neighbors and business associates who had just heard the news kept calling in to offer sympathy. There were reporters, who could be brushed off for now. But it was in the papers now anyway, and on TV. In the intervals between incoming calls, Lenore began phoning out, talking to relatives and old friends scattered around the country. As if it helped her, just to have the phone in her hand and talk. Andrew

didn't know where to look for something that
would help him. There was Judy, of course.
Thank God for Judy. She came and sat beside her
father, saying little, just being there.

Somewhere along the line Joe Keogh had departed. A time came when all the police were
gone. Lenore was on the phone, saying for what
sounded like the hundredth time: we don't know
yet about the funeral. After tomorrow, sometime.

Then the family made an attempt at gathering
for dinner. Andrew took over the phone, and rang
the Birches. "This is Andy. I think a son of mine is
over there?"

"Andy, good lord. Johnny was telling us . . .
it's so terrible. What can we say?"

"I guess there's nothing." Andrew hardly knew
any longer what he was saying himself. "Is John
there?"

"Why, no, he left some time ago. I think about
six. I thought he was going directly home, but he
might have stopped in at the Karlsens'."

"That's probably it." Andrew said goodbye,
hung up, and punched for the Karlsens' home.

But Johnny wasn't there either.

Phone cradled again, Andrew tried to think.
The Montoyas? They were in Mexico. Where else
might Johnny be? Somewhere in walking distance.

Andrew slipped on a coat and without saying
anything left the house and walked down the
long, curving drive. He felt there was no rational
reason for what he was doing, but he was not
going to let that stop him tonight. He noticed that
some stars were out. Could Johnny be standing
somewhere, gazing at them? The boy would do

that, sometimes. The telescope was put away, back in the small guest house near the lake.

As he walked down the drive he could hear distant surf behind him, smashing against the icefield, a different sound from that of its impact on rock and beach in summer. From in front came a murmur of light traffic, and passing headlights dazzled at him through the fir trees flanking his drive.

In the light of the next set of headlights Andrew saw that the flag on his mailbox had been raised. He himself had brought the Saturday mail in earlier in the day, and he had told the family often enough not to put anything out there over the weekend, not after that time when the checks were pilfered . . .

As he brought it back near the lighted house, Andrew's mind registered that the little brown-paper-covered package bore no stamps, and that it was addressed, ballpoint in an unfamiliar, clumsy block printing, to himself.

He carried it inside with him, and as Lenore approached, wondering out loud where he had been, he opened it. Paper fell away, revealing a box that had probably once held a gift pen. It opened easily.

Looking at the object inside, a freshly amputated finger with a ragged, bloody stump-end that had left blood-smears on the inner lining of the box, Andrew felt something like the beginning of comfort. In a moment he recognized the comfort as of the sort experienced when the nightmare goes too far, and one knows at last that one is dreaming.

Except that even in his dreams he had never

before heard Lenore, he had never heard anyone,
make noises like the ones that she was making
now . . .

An hour before midnight, with the drive again
full of police cars, Clarissa found herself rising
like a sleepwalker from her sleepless chair, moving away from the other members of her dis-
traught family and letting herself be drawn back
to the library.

Inside, she closed the door behind her, at the
same time switching on one light. The shelves at
the far east end were still in dimness.

In a pocket of her sweater her hand encountered
a handkerchief, which, come to think of it, was
part of her last year's Christmas gift from Johnny.
Dear God, let him be still alive! But it was too long
since she had genuinely tried to pray.

At the touch of her foot, the library stool glided
along the base of the shelves, then settled beneath
her modest weight to grip the carpet and hold
itself in place. Handkerchief in hand, she as-
cended to the second step. The seldom-disturbed
books on the top shelf must be dusty, given the
succession of part-time maids who had lately
been in charge of cleaning.

Clarissa whisked with the handkerchief, and
pocketed it again. Then her hand went out to the
book she wanted, one she had not opened in more
than thirty years.

November, 1946. Clarissa, widowed early in the
war, had been two years remarried to a Yank, John
Southerland, lately a brigadier in the US Eighth
Air Force. She was preparing to leave her native

England for her husband's home in far off Illinois;
one step in that preparation was to bid farewell,
for what had seemed would quite possibly be the
last time, to her grandmother Wilhelmina Harker.

The old lady had been in her seventies then,
though she looked no more than a well-preserved
sixty, and another two decades were to pass before she breathed her last. Eight years widowed
herself in 1946, Grandmother Harker was still living then in her turn-of-the-century home in Exeter. The house, like the rest of England, had been
left almost servantless by World War II, and was
in a gloomy, neglected state, with some of last
year's blackout curtains still in place.

Grandmother Harker had begun the interview
by looking keenly at little Andrew, who had ac-
companied his mother. "Will he be changing his
name to Southerland?" she demanded of Clarissa.

"I think he will." Clarissa's chin lifted, and her
tone balanced between defiance and toleration.
She had never spent much time with her grandmother and did not know her very well.

"Just as well," the old lady answered shortly, to
Clarissa's surprise. Then Grandmother Harker
had given the child his farewell present, a book of
adventure stories, had wished him well among all
the Red Indians in America, and then had sent
him off to play with some neighbor's offspring. It
turned out that the old woman had, or thought she
had, some very private business with Clarissa.

"When you come right down to it," Grandmother Harker said, waving at the younger
woman a fat, dark-bound book that Clarissa had
not noticed until that moment, "jewels and
money and such things are trivialities. At least

they are once one has enough of them to get along
in comfort. I understand your new husband is
quite well off?"

"Quite."

"Then I hope you won't be disappointed that
I'm not giving you anything of that sort."

Clarissa murmured a truthful denial, and at the
same time wondered: A book? What in the world?
She herself was not much of a reader, and certainly no collector; nor would she have guessed
her grandmother, who in her youth had been
rather adventuresome in a physical way, to have
any particular leaning in that direction.

The book was being extended steadily toward
Clarissa, in a slender hand that evidently still
retained surprising strength. The old lady said to
her: "But this is something valuable, my dear, as
such a parting gift ought to be. You know, you
were always my favorite among your generation
of the family. And now, why shouldn't I say so,
and do something to show I mean it? Truthfulness
is one of the few luxuries whose enjoyment becomes more practical as we grow older."

"A book." When the sound of her own voice
registered in Clarissa's ears she was afraid that she
had said it much too flatly. The book hadn't been
dusty on that day, though certainly it was already
very old. "How lovely!"

"You don't mean that, though you say it well.
Listen to me now. On the pages where I've put in
the marker, you'll find something much more useful than mere loveliness, should there ever come a
day of extraordinary trouble for you and your new
family."

Clarissa had accepted the book, and was making some remark appreciative of the old binding, when Grandmother Harker cut her off with a headshake and a sharp sigh. "I do hope I can make you understand me, girl. I've had this from the Continent at great—well, at great expense, though I don't mean of money but of effort. It wouldn't do for it to be forgotten, or ignored, or used with frivolity. No, that especially wouldn't do at all."

As far back as Clarissa was able to remember, her grandmother had somehow, from time to time, obtained impressive things "from the Continent". Lace, jewelry, at least once a fifteenth-century painting, later attested as a genuine Jan van Eyck by a surprised appraiser called in by the old lady herself, who must have had her own reasons to be suspicious of the acquisition. And Clarissa could recall, as a child, being introduced by grandmother to a dark, romantic-looking Continental gentleman of indeterminate age, come from that mysterious cross-Channel realm to visit grandmother, though grandmother even then, as even little Clarissa had been able to see, was rather ridiculously overage for such . . .

"Are you attending me, girl? Now when I speak of a day of extraordinary trouble, I certainly do not mean the simple deaths, diseases, cripplings; the common tragedies. Deserting husbands. Financial failures. Those God sends to us all."

Grandmother Harker leaned forward in her chair, and something in her eyes came so to life that Clarissa, a sensible woman of thirty-four who had come bravely through the Blitz and her first widowhood, involuntarily leaned away. The old woman went on: "I mean a day when the powers

of hell seem well and truly to have you in their
grip . . . use it then, and not before. And in God's
name, I say again, never in frivolity. I should
never dare to give it, if I thought it might be so
abused.''

"Use it?''

"Oh, don't be addle-pated! I can't abide that in a
girl with brains, of which you have a few, though
perhaps you don't like to use them. And while I
think of it, mind you go to church when you're in
America. There won't be Church of England, I
suppose, but go.'' Then, observing Clarissa's
trouble face, Grandmother Harker at last showed
pity. "Simply open the book to the marked page,
and do what it says. You remember your Latin,
don't you? Most of the ninnies who might open it
up by accident will not, I'm sure, which is a bless-
ing.''

"Thank you, Grandmother.'' In her own mind,
Clarissa lighted suddenly on the explanation—
though she was not entirely able to believe it—
that the old lady must have developed some
senile religious mania.

When she got home from the visit Clarissa
opened the old, old book and read the page
marked by a ribbon. She looked at the lock of hair
secured to the page by an incongruous strip of
cellophane tape, and tried to laugh. And then she
shut up the book for more than thirty years.

With the momentary feeling that those thirty
years had never been, she spread the thick book
open now, on a small library table of dark wood.
'You remember your Latin, don't you?' *Candel* at
any rate gave no trouble.

Nothing was said about using a particular kind of candle, and Clarissa went out of the library again, past a detective using the telephone in the hall, to extract a cherry-red taper from the Christmas centerpiece in the great empty dining room. Some matches from a holder near the elbow of the man still busy on the phone. Then back into her sanctuary. Candle in hand but still unlighted, she scanned the ancient print with the aid of bifocals and Tensor lamp.

As the door opened softly behind her, Clarissa started as if caught in a kidnapping herself.

It was Judy. Like the rest of the surviving household she was face-swollen and dazed. But she took one look at her grandmother and shut the door behind her.

"What are you doing, Granny?" The words were hushed; despite the open book the question was not, 'what are you reading?'

It crossed Clarissa's own dazed mind that in an earlier century Judy, in adolescence, would have been just ripe for witchery and hysteria. Perhaps that thought was what made Clarissa want her help. Or perhaps it was only a sudden fear of being left alone again that made the older woman beckon and put on a smile. "Come here, Judy. Help me read these words. I know you've had your schoolroom Latin, just as I did once."

Judy came to stand beside her. The old head and the young one, almost blond, bent over the old paper. A page cracked when it turned.

"What is it, Gran, an old prayer book?"

"About the closest thing to a prayer left in my life."

Each read in silence for a little while.

"It says to use a mirror, Grandmother." Not
Gran or Granny; not just now.

Clarissa did what passed for thinking in her
present state of shock. "Go fetch that small one
from the wall, down the hallway near your room."

Young legs in brown slacks, soft-shoed and silent, sprang away (something to be done at last!),
were back in only seconds.

Another minute or two of cooperation and
preparations were complete. Stacks of books held
the mirror propped vertically upon the table, so
that the pages of the old book, opened flat before
the mirror, were reflected. And now the words of
what was to be read aloud, printed in reverse,
sprang to legibility in the glass. The candle
burned, stuck clumsily with its own melted wax
to the fine wood of the table, and leaning a trifle
over the open book.

Now Clarissa pulled from the page the primi-
tive tape, which in thirty years had deteriorated
more than the old paper had in three hundred. It
came free easily, and immediately gave up into
her fingers the small lock of hair; mixed gray and
black. More resilient than either the paper or the
tape, as if it might have been trimmed off only this
morning. Whose? It did not look or feel at all like
Grandmother Harker's own brown-gray curls, as
Clarissa recalled them.

Side by side the candle flame and Tensor lamp
stared at their own reflections in the mirror.
Plenty of light, but the words would not come
clear for Clarissa. She started reading aloud,
stumbled, tried to make sense out of them. All
higgledy-piggledy nonsense, about the falling of
the sun, the rising of the night. More, just as ab-

surd. Not evil-sounding, no, not the black and evil thing—although right now she might have risked that too—for there in the text were the names of God and Jesus set down to be sworn by with respect. She could see that much, although the words all swam together now . . .

"Grandmother . . . lean back. Rest, please. Shall I read it for you?"

"Oh yes, my dear. It's so important. My own dear grandmother once told me . . ." Clarissa had to pause, or faint.

Judy put back the brown hair from her forehead, snapped off the Tensor, and in the candlelight leaned closer to the page and mirror. She gave a schoolroom clearing of the throat, and read through the passage twice: first in halting Latin; again in English translation that picked up speed as it went along.

" . . . walker by daylight, walker by night . . . come to my aid whose need is great . . ."

Remembering just in time, Clarissa leaned forward to do the other thing the ritual demanded. The candle flame sizzled, snapped at the dry morsels she fed it. The stink of burning hair stung at their nostrils.

And now there was nothing more for them to do. The rest was up to the unknown princely power whose aid they had besought; not God, to judge from the obscure text, but not Satan either. A saint?

Time passed, the girl standing straight now behind the old woman's chair, waiting to see if there was anything else that she could do for Gran. To Clarissa it seemed that a great silence now bound the house. The police must have departed once again, or most of them; some had planned to keep watch on the phones. Somewhere a jet, droning in across the lake, was heading for O'Hare.

"Granny, should I turn on another light?" The candle still burned, and one small bulb in a fixture near the door.

Already the spell that Clarissa in her desperation had tried to weave around herself was dissolving, like lake mist in the morning sun. Would God that it were morning already, instead of half the night still to be endured.

As the old woman raised herself from the chair, the joints of her knees and hips felt older than Grandmother Harker's had ever lived to be. "Judy, can you forgive me for all this nonsense? I'm a very foolish old—"

With a sharp sound the mirror, untouched by anything that either of the women could see or hear, smashed into a hundred pieces and crumpled in a heap of glass upon the table. Clarissa turned in time to see the candle, still half unburned, extinguish itself abruptly.

Five

Almost exactly sixteen hours, the traveler thought to himself, looking at his new wrist watch while the cab bore him, as he had directed, east and north from O'Hare Field. Here it was now four in the afternoon, and he should be just in time for tea, if one took tea in Illinois, which he was perfectly certain one did not. Sixteen hours from summons to arrival was not bad at all, considering all that he had had to do. My compliments, he thought, to BOAC. Of course he had long ago made preparations for some journey such as this—as he had for many other eventualities—and advance preparation always paid off when speed was essential.

"Turn east upon the next large road," he ordered, loudly and clearly, wondering exactly how his English sounded to the natives here. Of course he must sound basically British after so many years in London. The driver, a thick-necked black,

made a minimal motion of his head as if he was
moved to turn and argue with his passenger once
more that the best way to get where he was going
would be to confide the exact address of his des-
tination to such a professionally knowledgeable
guide as the driver himself. But the passenger's
reaction to argument last time had not been pleasant.

Actually the passenger did not know the exact
address he wanted, though he could feel the location of the place growing nearer. He momentarily
tilted his dark glasses aside with a long finger,
and squinted into dull sun-glow reflected from a
long roadside pile of thawing snow. It was a
dreary, soggy day, cloudy for the most part, not
really as cold as he had expected. "And now, if
you please, turn north again."

In another mile he had the man turn east, and
then in a little while, once more to the north. What
must be Lake Michigan, surprisingly oceanic at
first sight, hove into view upon the traveler's
right. He noted the appearance of the Shores
Motel, and regretted his lack of experience in
judging such establishments. A number of expensive cars were parked in front—of cars he knew a
little.

Not far, now. A few minutes later the traveler
was leaning forward in his seat, intently watching, thinking, feeling where he was being carried.
"Slow down. Slower! Now, take that next private
drive, there, upon our right!"

The man who answered the door was obviously
no servant; nor did the visitor take him for a
member of the family.

"Good day. I have come to see some members of the Southerland family."

The well-dressed man in the doorway was very watchful. "Can I ask the nature of your business, sir?"

"It is personal." But having by now recognized the other as some sort of policemen in plain clothes (this was a hopeful sign, suggesting that the difficulty for which he had been summoned was not trivial, or better yet that it had already been solved) the visitor handed over a card. "I am Dr. Emile Corday, an old friend of the family, just arrived from London."

Then he stood there on the doorstep, under polite police inspection, holding in mind just who he was supposed to be. Dr. Corday was an old family physician, retired now or on the verge. Basically a kind and comforting man, though with a crusty facade; could be irascible at times. He added: "I attended Mrs. Clarissa Southerland's grandmother in her last illness." It amused the visitor to be perfectly truthful in his deceptions when he could.

He was, as usual, convincing, and the plainclothesman stepped back. "Please, come in, Doctor."

Having already paid and dismissed the taximan, and being unencumbered by baggage, the visitor had nought to do but enter.

The examination, though, was not yet quite over. "Here, let me take your coat. You flew over from London just to see the family, did you?"

A woman of about forty-five, red-eyed and showing other signs of prolonged tension (another hopeful indication that he had not been forced to travel all this way for absolutely nothing) now appeared from deeper within the house, and exchanged glances with the policeman.

"I'm Lenore Southerland," she then informed the visitor, turning on him a gaze in which faint new hope and old terror were mingled.

Again he introduced himself as Corday, which name obviously meant nothing at all to her. Then, just as the policeman was on the point of interrupting with more questions, there appeared from another room a face that the visitor could recognize, given his developed talent for perceiving a child's features in the ruined mask of age.

And the recognition would perhaps be mutual. As soon as Clarissa's eyes (he had come up with her name a moment after her face clicked into proper focus in his memory) fell on him, it seemed from a certain tremor in their puffy lids, in concert with a preparatory sagging of her body, that she might be going to faint. He locked his eyes on hers—he had taken off the dark glasses when he came inside—and presently she rallied and stood straighter.

Ignoring the younger woman for the moment, he turned to Clarissa and took her hands in his and let her see a smile of reassurance. "Clarissa!" he greeted, in his best old-doctor voice. "It has been many years."

"Oh yes, it has," she breathed in answer, and that was enough to make the policeman retire for the time being. She went on: "You know—you've heard about our awful troubles here?"

"You shall tell me all about it right away." And, after a few minutes of polite and blurred conversation with daughter-in-law, he managed to get the aged woman to himself. Apparently having her own reasons to want to talk to him alone, she led him into what looked like a functioning library—and yes, there was the table the vision had shown him sixteen hours ago, complete with a speck of red candle-wax adhering to the darkly polished wood. On the carpet beside one table-leg there lay a minute sliver of broken glass.

The door closed by Clarissa's hand, they sat facing each other across the little table, he with his back to the windowful of winter daylight that now hung on as if it never meant to fade.

Neither of them spoke immediately. Clarissa's eyes, though she fought to keep them from doing so, flicked up once, twice, three times, to a high shelf behind him.

At last she had to say something. "You know, it's been so long . . . I'm afraid . . . I'm ashamed to have to ask, but—what is your name?"

"Corday," she repeated after him, mystified, when he had told it yet again. "Corday. Do you know, Doctor, I have the impression that I met you once when I was a small girl? I know that's . . . "

"In that impression I believe you are correct, Clarissa."

"But . . . no. Do you suppose that could have been your father?"

Now she was threatening to burble and gush. He sat in regal patience. Eventually he would hear more, learn more. Eventually he would confront his actual summoner, who had not yet appeared.

"It seems . . . it seems a strange coincidence that you should decide to visit us just now."

"It is nothing of the kind, my dear Clarissa, as I think you know full well. Where is the girl?"

Almost as if he had suddenly drawn a knife. "What girl?"

"An attractive young girl of seventeen or so dwells in this house. Last night—more precisely, about sixteen and one half hours ago—she sat in this room, at this table, with candle and mirror and a certain old book which is probably now on one of these high shelves behind me. I intend to see this girl and speak with her."

Clarissa's face was crumpling, along with the pretense that she had tried to maintain, that folk usually tried to maintain, that the world was a sane place whose basic rules they understood. She shook her head and moaned like someone choking on a bone. At last she got a few words out: "The mirror broke . . . I thought it might have been the candle's heat."

He waited silently.

"I—I hope I did the right thing." Her voice was very tiny now. Her eyes were those of a frightened bird.

"Indeed, I share your hope. I have affairs of my own, as you must realize, to which I should prefer to be attending." He sighed inwardly, wondering just how much Clarissa knew about him. Enough to scare her, obviously. "So, you instructed this girl—what is her name?"

"Judy." With a gulp.

"You instructed this young Judy in the means of summoning me."

"I was the one responsible. She only read the words."

"Only?"

Somewhere outside the library, male voices were droning, drearily determined.

"Clarissa, while I will do practically anything to please your dear grandmother, give every aid I can to anyone as near and dear to her as you are, I would not be amused to find my time and strength being wasted upon trivialities. So if this is a matter, say, of some stolen jewel, or perhaps some juvenile romantic difficulty—or even, God help us, a prank—let me warn you at once and bluntly that this family will be left the unhappier for my visit." He had seen indications already that things were more serious than that, but he wanted to make the point. "And in that depressing event I believe I can explain my actions to your grandmother so that she will understand."

There was a pause in which Clarissa could be seen marshalling reserves of strength. She sat up straight and looked him in the eye, almost for the first time. "Dr. Corday. My grandmother, Wilhelmina Harker? She died in 1967. She was ninety-five then."

Again the visitor fetched an inward sigh. "I am aware that in that year dear Mina ceased to breathe. That she was then consigned to her tomb . . . but we are straying from our business. Pray tell me, just what is the nature of this family difficulty which reddens every eye, and populates the house with such discreet policemen?"

The tale came out in a hurried, exhausted fashion. The granddaughter found mysteriously dead, yesterday morning. The grandson kidnapped last night, and mutilated for the pure hell of it, as it might seem; there was not even a ransom demand as yet.

Then someone exists who does such things to folk whom Mina loves. He nodded, showing little of what he felt. He might have been considering a strange problem in chess. "There is no doubt that the finger in the little package was cut from your grandson's hand?"

"They said it was—"

"What?"

"Not cut. More like—oh God, more like it had been torn from his hand. I didn't see it. But they had no doubt that it was Johnny's finger. He—he had a distinctive wart on it."

At least, mused the visitor, he is now free of that.

"And the police say that they believe that it was taken from a living hand. They have their scientific tests."

"To be sure. The finger must be still in their possession?"

"It must be. Yes."

"And the girl's body, too?"

"In the Chicago morgue, the medical examiner's office, whatever they call it. They're supposed to have the best facilities there for tests."

It was now time to be nice, and he startled Clarissa away from the brink of collapse by reaching across the little table and reassuringly pressing her fingers between his own. "It is a good thing that you and Judy called me."

"Good?"

"Yes, yes. I should have been angry if I were not called on in such a matter. Evil people have, for whatever reason, launched an assault upon your family. But soon it will be the turn of those wicked folk to be unhappy."

Although he smiled as he whispered those last

words, wanting them to be comforting, she pulled back.

He looked sharply over Clarissa's shoulder in the direction of the door. Two seconds later the door opened.

"Gran? Sorry, I didn't know you had company."

He heardly heard the girl's words, though. He found himself on his feet, with no memory of having risen, and staring at her uncontrollably. The first impression, which struck him like a club, was that Mina herself stood before him, young as when he had first met her, in the first flush of warmblooded, breathing life.

Yesterday's vision of his summoner had been no more than a passport photo, compared to this reality. The girl's clothing and hairstyle were of course of the late nineteen-seventies, not of eighteen ninety-one. But the face and the sturdy body and the bearing were Mina's—although at second glance, of course, not quite.

The girl was staring at him also—small wonder, given his reaction to her entrance. How long had it been since anything had caused him so to lose his self-possession? But thank heaven she did not seem frightened.

Clarissa had also risen to her feet. When she spoke her voice was calmer than the visitor had expected. "Dr. Corday? This is my granddaughter Judy. Judy, Dr. Corday has known the family for some time. He's just flown in from London."

"Your servant, my dear," the visitor murmured, smiling, and took the young girl's hand. He would

have felt the slightest pullback in her fingers, as
he bent to kiss the air above them in the old European style. But pullback there was none.

Some surprise, though, showed in her voice.
"You say that as if you meant it." Her voice was
jarringly American. Well, what else?

"I do."

Her brown eyes, Mina's eyes, probed at him
delightfully, trying to puzzle him out. "Doctor
Corday? Did I meet you in England, maybe? We
were over there in 1967. I'm sorry if I've forgotten,
but I was very young at the time."

"Of course you were. But we did not meet," he
said, releasing her hand regretfully. "It is impossible that I should not remember if we had."

Oh, those eyes of hers were, naturally enough,
not Mina's after all. So young and brown though,
and filled with puzzlement about him, and grief
for her mysteriously ravaged family. Intriguingly,
he could not find in them the personal fear that
marked the older women of the family.

Judy asked him gravely: "Are you staying with
us? I hope you can."

Clarissa rather lamely began to second this offer
of lodging, which the visitor declined with polite
firmness. "I shall be staying for some days in the
neighborhood, however, and I look forward very
much to visiting with you—with both of you. But
right now, child, I have a few minutes more of
urgent business with your grandmother . . . and,
Judy, dear? If your father is in the house, would
you ask him if he can spare a minute or two to talk
to me? Tell him his time will not be wasted—
thank you, Judy."

Watching the young girl leave, he marveled

once more at her likeness to his beloved. Then, with an energetic clapping and rubbing-together of his lean hands, he turned back to Judy's grandmother even as the old lady sank into her chair again.

"Now, my child," he whispered to her, bending closer to her ear. "How have your dear son and his lovely wife managed to acquire such demonic enemies? You can tell me—you must tell me—the truth."

At this Clarissa began to weep. Which, as the visitor could see, was not something she did easily or frequently. "You must believe me," she told him between gulping sobs. "I have no idea."

He looked at her closely, and patted her hands again. "I do believe you. And now, can you arrange for me to have a word in private with your son? Don't tell him that I want to question him, of course."

"Question him? Question him? Why must you do that?"

"Because I have been brought here to help him. To help all of you. It is all out of your hands now, my dear. Let me go about things in my own way."

Clarissa spent a little longer in sniffling recovery from her tears, thinking about this. "I never thought that old book . . . ."

"Ha. Why then did you use it?"

"What is it that you want me to tell my son?"

"That I would like to speak with him—there must be something in which his interest can innocently be caught. By which he may be distracted a little from his grief and worry. He has perhaps a hobby that fascinates him? Chess, photography . . . ?"

"Pottery," said Clarissa in a very low voice. Almost completely recovered from her weeping now, she was looking at the visitor with such a guarded, watchful, poker-playing stare that he really had to smile.

"Clar-iss-a! Was your grandmother such a terrible enemy of yours? Would she have delivered you and your own beautiful grandchild into the devil's hands? No, no, no, you must know better than that."

"Then who are you? Really?"

He emphasized the first words of his smiling answer with little hand-pats, delivered on alternate syllables. "I am Dr. Emile Corday, of London, an old friend of the family, and no one, no one, can prove anything to the contrary. Now, will you choose to help me? Or to help the creatures who have torn off your grandson's finger?"

Six

"Andrew? Dr. Corday is very interested in pottery. He was wondering if you might have time to show him a little of your collection before dinner."

Clarissa and the visitor had come upon Andrew standing in the hallway, gazing at a phone on a small table as if he knew or hoped that it was about to ring. Introductions had been brief.

"He's really interested. Go along, dear, it'll do you good to think of something else."

"All right, Mother." With a last pensive glance toward the phone, Andrew turned away from it. A minute later, Clarissa having effaced herself, he was guiding the visitor toward the rooms where, as he said, most of the things were currently being kept.

This proved to be in an obviously older wing of the house, a one-story extension running north from what was now the main building. The origi-

nal style of construction of this old wing had been
partially obliterated by extensive remodelling
carried on (as near as the visitor could guess)
some decades back, and survived mainly in
pseudo-Gothic archways separating rooms, gray
stone walls still showing here and there, and
some tall, narrow windows well suited to the
needs of defending bowmen.

"Most of the collection is in this room, Doctor."

And now they were standing in the midst of it.
The large chamber held not only pottery of almost
every conceivable age and provenance, but a jumble of other old things as well. There were two
suits of what looked to the visitor like authentic
medieval armor. On side walls were some large,
second-rate old Flemish tapestries. But he looked
most intently at the wall opposite the door, where
there hung a portrait of Mina herself.

"That is intriguing, isn't it, Doctor? My wife's
grandmother, on the Harker side of the family. But
of course you probably know . . . it was done by
Gustav Klimt. Nineteen-oh-one, I think."

The old man could not now recall the date with
any certainty either, though he well recalled the
sunlit sitting room in Exeter where Mina had
posed for this painting, and his own quick exit
from that room into the noonday sun, with perilously aching eyes, on a day when Mina's husband
and the artist had come home sooner than expected. And sure enough, there was gray stodgy
Jonathan, still intruding in the only way that he
could manage now, just down the wall from Mina
in an inferior portrait done sometime in the 'twen-
ties.

"You see, Doctor, we Southerlands are one of

those American families who were involved around the turn of the century in what some people think of as the looting of poor old Europe by vulgar young America. That was when some of us here had a lot of money, and a lot of the old European families didn't. It was possible to buy up . . . but I keep forgetting, you probably know all that better than I do."

"*That* was not looting, dear sir. Not at all."

"This incense burner is Chinese porcelain, of course. Wan Li reign. But it came here through Europe." Southerland went on, evidently seeking whatever distraction he might be able to find here, for there was a dry eagerness in his voice. "Of course we've added in more recent decades, recent years . . . this terra-cotta sarcophagus here was sent over during the war. There was a lot of space available in ships westbound from England in those days, I understand. I myself no longer work at collecting as I once did . . . and this little black bowl is Santa Clara Pueblo . . . Kate was starting to get interested in the Indian things . . ." Eagerness gone, slumping against a table, Andrew paused, as if suddenly exhausted.

"How easy it is," the visitor observed, "particularly in the world of business, for an innocent man to acquire terrible enemies."

"Enemies?" Southerland did not seem greatly surprised at the suggestion; still he thought about it for a while, as if it had never occurred to him before. "Yes, we all make them, don't we, and without even trying. The police have asked me several times: who are your enemies? Any servants with a grudge? Hell, we haven't had any really regular help in the house in years. Servants come and go. They don't even remember who we are half the time, much less hate us."

"I know how difficult it can be to confide in the police."

"What I just can't understand is this happening to a boy like John. Not like some of these other kids, pot-smoking, getting girls in trouble. A little driving trouble once, last fall, was all I ever had with John." Southerland's countenance convulsed, as if he were trying with all the muscles of his face to squeeze something out of himself. "And Kate," he added brokenly, and put his face down in his hands.

"I am a father too, you know." The visitor's voice was soft, though without perceptible emotion. "Or I was."

"I didn't know," said Andrew, as if it couldn't matter. He looked up, starting to recover from his spasm.

"Not many do. But you are quite right, my family affairs are neither here nor there. Tell me, have you any dealings with what I believe is locally called the Mafia?"

"What? Never." Southerland's reddened eyes, now shocked anew, probed at the visitor. "Who said a thing like that about me?"

"No one, to my knowledge. But if you cannot guess who the guilty parties may be, then I must try to do so."

"You?" Southerland blinked at him stupidly, but aggressively. "What have you to do with this?" When the visitor stood silent, his host went on, now in a conciliatory tone: "Forgive me, I don't mean to insult any old friend of Mother's. But I've gone through all these same questions with the police. I don't know why my children are being attacked. If I knew, don't you suppose . . . I just don't know."

The visitor found himself beginning to be convinced of this. But he said nothing, only turned instead to watch the Gothic doorway leading to the hall, where two seconds later there appeared the figure of a man.

The newcomer was about thirty, sparely muscular, tough-faced, fair-haired, dressed with classless American informality in boots, jeans, and a plaid jacket over a plaid shirt of different pattern. He favored the old man with a quick but judgemental glance that to the latter once more suggested the police. But when he spoke it was to their host: "Andy? Judy said you were back here. I just wanted to tell you—God, what can anyone say?"

Andy—the European visitor could not really manage to think of him by that name—pressed his lips together and shook his head and looked away. So it was left to the old man to break a slightly awkward pause, which he did by putting out a cordial hand. "I am Dr. Emile Corday, an old friend of Clarissa's grandmother."

"I heard about you from Clarissa. Pleased to meet you." The young man's grip was firm, though probably moderated in consideration of Dr. Corday's age. "I'm Joe Keogh, Kate and I were . . . " Glancing toward Kate's father, he let his words trail off.

"I understand. Well, Andrew?" Trying to fit the American style, he could just about manage *Andrew*. "Shall we all rejoin the ladies?"

Southerland agreed spiritlessly and came with

them, walking now as if he were the aged one of the group. "If you don't mind, gentlemen, I think I'm going to lie down for a while . . . Lenore?" They had just re-entered the newer portion of the house, where his wife met them. "Will you call me at once if anything important comes up?"

"Of course. Lie down if you like." His wife, hardly looking at any of them, seemed as distracted as before. "Dr. Corday? Joe? You're both going to stay to dinner, aren't you?"

Corday bowed neatly. "Much as it would please me, Lenore, I cannot. Tomorrow I should like to drop in again, and talk over old times with Clarissa. And of course to do what I can to lighten the burdens on you all. Meanwhile, messages can reach me at the Shores Motel."

Joe in turn made vague excuses for not staying, and then put forward the offer, quickly accepted, to drop off Dr. Corday at the Shores. Lenore did not press either of them to remain. Judy, rejoining them at the last moment, did, but desisted when she saw that both really preferred to leave.

Outside, walking backwards into a gust of wind that howled across the floodlit gravel drive, Joe Keogh had a considerate eye out for the old man's footing. "Watch out, kind of icy here with these frozen puddles."

The old man wondered for a moment if his arm was going to be taken. But that indignity did not occur, and he followed Joe among the parked cars of family members and the police—some of whom were still in the house, listening for ransom demands at one of the telephones. Joe's vehicle, a small, gray German import, was the most modest of the lot.

They had driven perhaps half a mile south on Sheridan Road, here fronted mostly by the driveways, walls, and gates of other set-back mansions, before the old man spoke again: "You grieve for her deeply." Probing, he put a kind of challenge into the words.

The driver glanced over at him. "I do." He paused. "Do they get this kind of weather much in your part of Europe?"

"You have noticed my accent, which I fear still betrays my central European origins. And my French name, of course. But I really do now make my home in London, where these days cold this intense and snow this heavy are rare. Now I see that you do grieve, indeed. Even though you were never formally betrothed, I take it?"

Joe let a little time and traffic go by. "There were difficulties about that. Maybe you noticed, Kate's parents aren't exactly crazy about me. I felt like I was engaged to her, though she hadn't actually said she'd marry me. You know?"

"You had, perhaps, a rival?"

"That wasn't it." Pause. "She . . . just hated to give up her freedom." A longer pause. "Some of her wealthy acquaintances must have wanted to marry her too."

"Which ones?"

"I wouldn't know." Again snow was falling, a flurry of stray white blurrings in the slow-moving headlights.

"You are not wealthy, then."

"No, I'm just a Chicago cop." Joe felt his lips quirk in a smile half a second in duration. "Some people in my line have gotten wealthy, but I doubt I ever will."

"I suppose you have not been assigned any official part in Kate's case? Or her brother's?"

"The specialists will do a better job. I'm in the Pawnshop Detail: recovering stolen merchandise, things like that. Right now they've given me a few days off."

The road curved, and its new angle had been blown clean by some trick of the wind. Now the houses flanking it on both sides were less monumental, the driveways shorter.

"See," said Joe, "I don't have much family." He cleared his throat and tried again. "I belong to this kind of Catholic social club for single people. Kate got into it too. Sometimes the people in the club go to hospitals, children's homes, and so on, do a little volunteer work. I met her on one of those deals . . . here we are, Shores Motel."

But when the car had stopped, in a splendor of light from the signs and windows of the ornate office, the old man made no immediate move to get out. He just sat there, looking at Joe so regally that Joe wondered for a moment if the chauffeur was expected to get out and walk around and open the door for the distinguished passenger.

But it turned out that his passenger had only been mulling over another question. "Do you know where poor Kate's body is at present?"

"The Chicago morgue. Why?" Joe was suddenly a little angry at this pointless nosiness. He shifted in his seat to face the other more fully. The lights from the motel showed Corday's chin smooth-shaven, lean and firm despite the lines of age. The mouth was tough in a thin-lipped way, beneath a mildly beaky nose. The eyes above were still in shadow, though lights made motionless spots of bright reflection in them. Joe thought suddenly: I would not want this old man for my enemy.

The thin-lipped mouth said: "Determination of the cause of death has long been something of a specialty of mine. Would you be kind enough to drive me to the Chicago morgue tonight? Or at least give me the address?"

"Tonight?"

The old man nodded, minimally.

"Doctor, I don't know what kind of hours they keep in Europe, but they're not going to let any strangers into that place tonight."

Corday's mouth smiled solidly. "But I should like to see the building, at least, that I may know where it is. And I am eager to discover something of the great city near us; and eager also to continue our so-interesting conversation. Would it be a great inconvenience, for you to drive me there?"

"They're not going to let you in," Joe explained, with what he felt was beautiful patience.

"Or would you prefer to go to your home, and brood alone upon life's sadnesses?"

The morgue was a little south of the Loop, only a couple of blocks from central police headquarters on State. After driving past both buildings, Joe found a vacant parking space about halfway between them, on a street of tall office buildings all locked up and darkened for the night. He needed a parking space because it seemed that he was going to have to do a little more patient explaining still.

"Look, Dr. Corday, you're a real good listener, for which I'm grateful. It's been a help talking to you. But as far as trying to get into that place tonight, it's silly. They won't let us in just because I'm a cop or you're a doctor."

"I ask only that you wait here in the car for a few minutes, Joe, if you would be so kind. I shall walk back to the building myself."

Joe shook his head. "Maybe you can just walk around London alone at night, I wouldn't know. Here it isn't always safe—ah!"

The stubborn old man had started to get out. Joe, determined to use gentle force if necessary to make him behave sensibly, had taken him firmly by the coatsleeve. It wasn't reasonable that the old man's flesh could really have delivered a stinging electric shock to his hand through the thick cloth. But that was what it had felt like. Rubbing his thumb and fingers together now, testing for injury, Joe could feel nothing wrong. He must have somehow twinged a nerve or twanged a tendon.

By now the old man was standing at his ease outside the re-closed door. "I shall be quite safe," he murmured with a smile, and touched his dark hatbrim. He turned away and in a moment long strides had taken him around a corner.

All right, the chances were, of course, that nothing would happen. Winter nights were safer than summer ones on the streets of the core city, and the streetlighting here was excellent. But to a stranger, a perhaps innocent foreigner, there was a special responsibility.

Joe got out of the car on his side, buttoned up his jacket, and walked to the corner, flexing the fingers of his right hand. They felt fine, now. He would catch up with the difficult old man and walk along. How did he get into these things? But at the same time he was relieved not to be home alone in his apartment.

He stood at the corner, squinting thoughtfully down a long, broad sidewalk almost empty of pedestrians. The old man was nowhere in sight.

Seven

The visitor stood alone in a dark room, halfway
along a broad, terrazo-floored aisle that was lined
on both sides with double tiers of massive metal
drawers. In the next room, the possessor of a pair
of middle-aged male lungs was sitting in a
slightly squeaky chair, sitting quite still and on
the verge of snoring. The light coming under the
closed door from the room where the watchman
dozed was all that the visitor had to let him see the
tags on the drawers, but it was more light than he
needed. What handicapped him in his search was
not darkness but the impenetrable official jargon
on the tags, labels for this foreign city's mysterious dead. Presently, with an almost inaudible hiss
of relief, he gave up trying to be methodical—
never his strong suit anyway—and slid a long
drawer out at random.

The sheet-draped body in it was that of an adolescent black male whose forehead had been

grossly damaged, the rest of the face less so, by some violent flat impact. Automobile, pavement, weapon? Touching the dark marble shoulder, the visitor still could not be sure of which. But the physical contact established for him some rapport. Not only with this one truncated identity, but, by some dimly perceived extension of the contiguity, with all the silent company about.

That was a start. The old man slid the young black statue back out of sight and stood with closed eyes in the near-dark, concentrating deeply. Now he began to pace along the aisle, brushing his long fingers on the cold handles of the drawers. Top row, bottom row, top again . . . he knew without pulling them open that in one was a woman, somewhat too old to be the girl he wanted, in the next, a man, another man, a boy, a girl . . . .

Even before the chosen drawer flowed out on easy rollers at his touch, he was quite sure that he had found Kate Southerland. His hand went out to delicately turn back the rim of coarse white sheet from the face of Judy's sister.

The revealed face froze him into immobility.

For the second time in as many hours he found himself taken completely by surprise. All his delicately forming plans, estimations, guesses, regarding the Southerland affair, every theory that he had begun to play with in his mind, all vanished like the rising mist at dawn.

This was not true death before him.

Oh, the girl was cold and unbreathing certainly, her heart as quiet as her hands: medical student and expert pathologist alike would certify her dead. But the old man was able to perceive the

energies of altered life that still charged all this
pretty body's cells. Again he drew a minimal
breath, and uttered that faint, almost reptilian
sound, expressing to himself his own surprise.
Had she enemies so bitter that they meant her to
be autopsied alive?

Or . . .

He passed his flat, extended hand once close
above the girl's face, forehead to chin. Then he
made the same motion in reverse. He needed only
the one pass to make Kate's eyes open for him.
They were unseeing as yet, but a lovely milk-blue,
glass-blue, in the night.

It was important to know whether there had
been any attempt at autopsy as yet, and imperson-
ally he drew the sheet down farther. The virgi-
nally flat belly was marked by no incision. Good.

With doctorly gentleness he drew the sheet up
to just below Kate's chin. Then he pressed with
two fingers on her cheek to turn her head. As he
did so he murmured tremendously old words, in a
language that could find keys of understanding
within the inner levels of almost every human
mind. The rigor of Kate's muscles eased somewhat. Her head turned, her eyelids drooped again,
and simultaneously she smiled. *What did you tell
me, old man? Something nice.*

He smiled too, for a moment, seeing a trace of
Mina's lineage before him in the smooth generous
forehead and lips. Oh, this was Judy's sister, yes,
though older, blonder and blander, and by his
own standards not so beautiful.

The expert pathologist would almost certainly
never have thought of looking for the marks
which the old man, knowing just where to look,

could now observe upon the throat. A pair of less-than-pinprick wounds, now almost closed. By their spacing he knew that a wide human jaw had bitten there.

Next, with one finger the old man parted Kate's cold lips and explored her teeth. The four cuspids all responded somewhat like erectile tissue to his touch; what had once been inert enamel sharpening visibly.

He pressed her hand. "Look at me, Kate!" No more than a whisper was his voice, and yet a fierce command. And when her milk-blue, innocent eyes turned toward him he bent a little, whispering more intently still: "Who is your secret lover?"

Kate's smile failed, and a tremor ran through her upper body. To give the required answer meant drawing breath for speech, and breath to her was no more an automatic reflex. After a moment of awkward agony her lungs worked once, and she got out one word: "No—"

No secret vampire lover, it would seem, had left her in this state. Some vampire rapist, then. The old man's whisper lost its gentle undertone, came out between thin lips as though from a machine: "Who forced himself upon you, then?"

A difficult gasping. "Enoch . . . Winter . . . ."

The name meant nothing to the old man. "How long have you known him?"

"Just . . . met . . . "

"He bit at your throat; I can see that for myself. Forced you to taste his blood as well, perhaps?" Otherwise it was unlikely that a single mating would have brought about her transformation.

Ugly remembrance dawned in Kate's dull eyes;

she answered with a soundless yes. Her rib cage labored, but pumped little air. It was not surprising that her strength was low; the newborn vampire could be as weak, though hardly as fragile, as the infant newborn in the breathing phase of life. The visitor squeezed Kate's hand as he had squeezed Clarissa's, and made himself smile reassuringly. "I am an old friend of your grandmother's, Kate. Only one more question now, and you may sleep again. Where is John?"

"John . . ."

Now even the old man needed his best efforts to hear her. "Your brother. Is he with Enoch Winter?"

A faint line of puzzlement creased Kate's otherwise flawless forehead. He got the impression that she knew nothing of her brother's fate.

"All will be well now, Kate. Rest, sleep, until I come for you. Answer no call but mine. No call but mine. We will have much to talk of, later. But for now, rest."

And yet her lungs continued laboring to breathe, to get out one more word. He bent lower, intent on hearing.

"—Joe—"

For six minutes Joe Keogh had been back in the driver's seat, with engine and heater running, keeping a sharp eye out for the old man and wondering when he should really begin to be alarmed. Now Joe started, with almost the sensation of electric shock repeated. His companion was standing once more beside the car, where he seemed to have reappeared while in the very act of reaching for the door handle. What good would you be in a stakeout? a part of Joe's mind demanded angrily of himself. And another part answered: I *was* watching. He just—just—

"I told you you wouldn't be able to get in," he said aloud, with irritation, meanwhile reaching across the front seat to flip the doorlatch up.

"You were quite right," replied Corday in a soothing, almost contrite voice, as he slid in and closed the door. "The attendants were not at all inclined to be helpful. One of them was sleeping at a desk. A most ill-run establishment. Were I in charge, things would be different there."

Joe sighed, trying to remember if you could see anyone's desk from outside the front door of the morgue. "I'll take you back to your motel."

"If that is out of your way I can easily take a cab."

Joe shifted into drive and moved out, north on State, then swinging east to get back to the Outer Drive. "No problem, I'm headed back to the north side anyway." He hadn't really been headed that far north, but what the hell. Anyway there was something about the old man, in spite of all his oddities—or maybe because of them—that made Joe reluctant to let go of him. An air of hope; maybe that was it. A feeling of purpose, which was more than Joe had been able to get from anyone else around him since Kate's death. Looking at the ugly situation logically, of course, there wasn't much to be hopeful or purposeful about—except the chance of recovering Johnny still alive, and to Joe that chance looked smaller and smaller as the hours passed.

His companion's voice, breaking in upon his thoughts, was welcome. "Tell me one more thing,

Joe, if you know it. What are the plans for Kate's burial?"

"As far as I know, no time's been set. Waiting on the autopsy, which is supposed to be tomorrow. I'm sure she'll be buried up in Lockwood Cemetery, in the family mausoleum. It's one of those the really wealthy Chicago families liked to put up around the turn of the century: all marble and as big as a middle-sized house. One of those famous architects designed it, I forget his name."

"Thank you, Joe. You have been very helpful to me tonight." It was said so sincerely that it sounded a little odd.

Joe glanced at the once-more shadowed face. "You'll be coming to the funeral, then."

"At my age," the old man said calmly, "it is difficult to know which funerals one will be able to attend."

Eight

When the closet door was closed Johnny never tried to open it, not after that first time, even though sometimes the house grew so silent that he could imagine himself alone in it.

On his first night in the closet all had been silent, for what seemed like an endless time, and at last he had eased the door open with his good hand, thinking maybe they had somehow left him unguarded. The huge man had been right there in the dark empty bedroom, standing right there as if he had been waiting hours for Johnny to do just that. That was when the huge man, without saying a word, had torn off the little finger on Johnny's right hand.

The little finger on his left hand had gone even sooner, while he was still in the kidnap-car and trying to struggle. He had fainted, and when he came out of the faint—he couldn't tell how much later—he found himself already here, shut up naked in the closet.

In the car, the huge man had ridden in the back seat, and the black-bearded man had done the driving. Black-beard was the one who had first beckoned Johnny over to the car as if to ask directions of him. When you were the fourth best high school wrestler in the state at a hundred and sixty pounds, you didn't fear any more that some maniac could just grab you like a baby and throw you into the back seat of a car.

It had turned out, though, that someone could.

Then there was the man with the thick glasses, a short and muscular and sometimes nervous young man. He had not been in the car at all, but he stayed with Johnny in the house, escorted him from closet to bathroom and back again, and put food and water in the dishes on the closet floor.

Also there was the woman. Johnny was not quite sure, in his state of pain, fever, shock, fear, and confusion, whether he was dreaming her or not. He heard her sometimes; he never saw her clearly. She had not been in the car either. Once she came to the closet door and opened it, in darkness so thick that even his now fully adjusted eyes could see nothing but the vague outline of her body. Then she had bent forward to touch him, with a finger or perhaps a toe, as he lay on the floor. And she had laughed, musically, and had spoken to someone who was over near the door that must lead from the bedroom to a hall. Her language sounded a little like Latin, but mostly like nothing that Johnny had ever heard before. Then she had gone away again.

It was not easy to keep track of time. In the bedroom outside the closet, a modern but abandoned-looking room with no furniture that he traversed on his escorted trips to the bathroom, the drapes were always closed. Still he could just tell whether it was daylight outside or not. The trouble was in sorting out the periods of day and night and keeping track of how many of them had passed. And there was more trouble in trying to believe there was a reason why he should bother to keep track at all.

Thick-glasses sometimes left him plain bread in the aluminum pie plate placed on the luxuriously carpeted floor. Once there was cheese with the bread, and once it had turned into a peanut butter sandwich. Johnny didn't eat much, whatever it was. He did drink a lot of water, though, out of the other dish. Lapping it up was the best way, because then he didn't have to use his hands at all. They both hurt so much he wasn't going to try to use them except to save his life. Maybe not even then.

It might have been his second night in the closet when he heard the car pull up outside. Immediately Thick-glasses went into a flurry of activity, entering the bedroom from somewhere, momentarily pulling aside the drapes to look out, then opening the closet door to growl: "Make any noise and it'll be your left nut that comes off next." Then he closed the door and went trotting off somewhere, closing the bedroom door too behind him.

Johnny could hear nothing more for several minutes. Then two sets of footsteps entered the bedroom, its ceiling light was switched on, the closet door was opened. Even with his eyes dazzled, Johnny could recognize Black-beard from the kidnap car.

The two men stood there looking at him on the floor. Black-beard was wearing some kind of fancy winter jacket with snow on the collar. Thick-glasses wore his usual khakis, almost a uniform.

"If the plan's going on," said Black-beard, "we don't want him to die yet; we'll want to send some more parcels. He's shivering, better get him a blanket."

"Oh, the plan's going on," Thick-glasses said.

Black-beard: "I'd like to get it straight about this house, who owns it, how secure it really is."

"She's taking care of all that."

They closed the closet door. Their voices stayed in the lighted bedroom, though.

"Look, man." It was Black-beard talking again. "You've really known her longer than I have, right? Her and her big friend. It was really you who arranged for her to meet me, huh?"

The other was quiet for a few moments. "Yeah." As if he didn't want to talk about that.

"I'm going to have to talk to her, get a few things straight. Like who really decides things. Meanwhile I want you to understand that I'm the one who does."

"Sure."

"I'm not gonna hang around here. Do either of them ever come out here?"

"They haven't yet."

"What'd you do with his clothes?"

"I got 'em stashed away. This way he's not gonna go running out. Also I don't have to do his zipper for him."

Black-beard chuckled. "Makes something else a little handier for you too, hey?"

"Hey, you know I don't like to touch no one who's unhealthy." Thick-glasses sounded genuinely hurt. "He's all blood and shit—yuck."

"You could give him a bath."

"Come on, get off me, Boss."

"All right, all right." Black-beard quenched his amusement. "Look, Gruner, you're doing a fine job here, a helluva job. I'll get word back to you on what to do next. You sure the phone here's not connected?"

"Sure."

Their voices moved away.

Later that same night—though Johnny could not be quite sure it really was the same night—he swam up out of sleep or stupor to hear that a party was in progress. Not in the bedroom; somewhere farther off. Voices again speaking that language that was almost Latin—this time maybe half a dozen people, having what sounded like a quiet good time. Eventually he could pick out the voice of the woman who had looked in on him the night before. He didn't hear Black-beard's, though, or Thick-glasses' either.

Some strange man's voice said, impatiently: "Oh, speak English here, why don't you?" Impatience was smeared over with good-humor, to make it sound polite.

And then the lovely voice of the woman who had looked in on Johnny, answering in English: "I have lived on this side of the ocean for two years now. I know the custom. I choose to disregard it, usually. But if the mother tongue is hard for you, I will use English, as a favor."

Another woman said: "If you're doing favors, I take it that you want something; you've called us together to ask our help. You have brought your feuds here from across the sea. That boy in the closet is connected with it somehow, I'm sure."

Several voices murmured agreement. The anonymous woman went on: "Well, we want nothing to do with any of that. Here there is no real knowledge of us among the breathers. No persecution ever, nothing but jokes. We wish things to remain as they are on this side of the water."

"Au contraire," replied the woman with the lovely voice, now more silken than ever. "I only offer you my friendship. I do not ask your help. What lies between the old one and myself is our own affair, not yours at all."

"That's fine with us," a second man put in.

"I have claimed no titles or honors here among you, have I?"

"Nor has he—you say he is here now, too."

"He is here. And you may be sure that he will claim honors—and obedience—if he wins. But all I ask is that you leave it to ourselves to settle." The fine voice paused. "No, let me be plainer than that. I insist that you give him no help, and above all no place of sanctuary. Any of you who dare to do so will feel our wrath in days to come. His time is past, and none should look to him for leadership."

"I hope that all of you are listening," said the huge man's voice, rough and elemental, like something from a thundercloud. And Johnny felt the world slip from him into darkness.

Nine

More often than not, Judy slept with the drapes of her bedroom window drawn open, and so it was tonight. Starlight and moonlight from the high sky above the lake were welcome, and dawn too, on the rare occasions that it roused her. There was no reasonable way that any human being could look in, on the second story. So when she awoke, near midnight, she wondered for a moment if it could be some trick of starlight from the new-cleared sky that made it appear that the old man, yesterday's brief visitor, was sitting in her dressing-table chair.

"Have I frightened you, Judy?" The voice of the apparition was quite matter-of-fact.

"No, I don't scare easily." Actually she was beginning to wonder if she was dreaming. Judy turned to face her visitor more directly as she sat up in her bed. Automatically her hands pulled sheet and blanket up close beneath her chin, and she felt her fingers touch her nightgown's throat, to make sure that it was buttoned. "But how did you get in?"

"I was invited, yesterday, into this house. And in my case one invitation is enough, you see. It has a permanent effect."

"I don't think I do see." But truly she was not afraid of him. She wondered a little, now, and later was to wonder more, about this lack of fear.

"Of course I have not been invited into your room. Shall I apologize for being here?"

"No, I don't mind. That is, I suppose you must have some good reason."

The old man made a little hissing sound not quite a sigh, and shifted in his chair. "I need a little help. I thought of waking Clarissa—but when I remembered your delightful lack of fear yesterday afternoon I came to you instead."

"A good thing you did. Gran's had angina. But what was there yesterday afternoon to be afraid of?"

This time the little hiss was almost a chuckle. "People can be very timid. Sometimes they are even afraid of me. Believe it or not."

"Why?"

"And one might think that these monstrous attacks upon your family would frighten you. Your mother and grandmother are both terrified, and your unhappy father is at the end of his wits, as the saying goes."

"Oh, it's not really that I'm so brave. It's . . ." Judy had to pause. She had never really tried before to put into words the way she dealt with fear. "It's just that when you're *really* scared, the only thing to do is try to go beyond the fear somehow. Accept it, maybe that's what I mean. And then go on your own way regardless." Now that she had found words, they did seem right, or almost right, to her. She would not have expected someone else to understand them, though.

But the old man was leaning forward in his chair, nodding. " 'Go on your own way, regardless.' I think it wonderful that you, at your age, already understand that. It does not, of course, imply a freedom from moral responsibility."

His voice had a marveling intensity that made Judy feel uncomfortable. She asked: "What is it you need help with?"

"Help? Ah, yes." The old man leaned back in his chair, and gave his little sigh. "I want some of Kate's clothing. A complete outfit will be best."

"What for?"

"Questions will not help me in what I am trying to do. The clothing may."

Judy considered for a moment, then swung legs swathed in a long, chaste winter nightgown out of bed. She groped with her toes for slippers. "A complete outfit. Underwear too?"

"Everything, please. As if you were helping her get dressed."

"All right. Wait here." Belting a robe around her, Judy went out of her room and down the familiar upstairs hall to Kate's. There she rummaged mechanically in drawers and closet. What am I doing here? she thought. I'm definitely awake now. Was I dreaming, after all, a minute ago? Will he still be there when I get back?

Trusting her instincts, she finished gathering the clothes before she hurried back to her own room. The old man waited for her, solid as the chair he sat on, dressed as he had been yesterday in a black topcoat over a dark suit. His soft, dark hat was in his lap.

"Here," said Judy. "I even got a bra, though more often than not Kate doesn't wear one."

"Ah," said the old man. The word was not exactly embarrassed, but perhaps he didn't know just what to say. He got up from his chair and held open a small, dark bag that Judy had not noticed before. Into it she dropped the clothing bundle. "Now," he said, tucking the bag under one arm, "since we are co-operating so well, do you suppose it might be possible to obtain the key to the family mausoleum in Lockwood Cemetery?"

"What for?" Again she asked the question automatically. But this time thinking it over only confirmed her right to ask. Hands jammed in the pockets of her robe, she stood waiting for an answer.

The old man seemed to think his answer over carefully before he gave it. "Your father mentioned to me that some of the larger and, ah, less costly pieces of his pottery collection have been relegated to that mausoleum. Should he ever question you about the key, you might mention that you gave it to me so I could look at those items without intruding any more upon his grief. Of course, if he never notices that the key is gone, we need not bother him about the matter at all. Would you concur?"

"You have a neat way of not answering questions."

"Would you concur?"

"I guess so. Dr. Corday?"

"Yes?"

The question Judy really wanted to ask would not quite come out, even when she tried to tell herself again that she might be dreaming. Instead she said: "I think I know where Father keeps all the keys we don't use much. On a big key ring in his desk in the study. They're all tagged, or most of them are. But I'm pretty sure the desk is locked."

Her visitor smiled at her. He had a nice smile. "In that case we need not worry about it tonight. I shall ask him for the key another time."

"Dr. Corday?"

"Yes."

"Is Kate alive?" Now it was out.

For once it seemed he could not find an answer he was happy with. "Would you believe me, child, if I said she was?"

"Don't call me a child, please. Do you think I am one?"

"No." He bowed, fairly deeply. "I am sorry. No, I do not think that at all. I would not have wasted half an hour from my duties, sitting here, to watch a child sleep."

What he had just said was something that Judy did not want to have heard; and anyway she did not want to be distracted. "Give me an answer. *Is* she?"

He studied her in silence.

Judy pressed on. "I've dreamed about her. Last night, and again tonight, before you came. In the dream I see her alive, but locked up somewhere. She keeps calling for Joe, but he can't hear her. And now you ask me for the mausoleum key, and for her clothes. Why do I trust you? But I do."

"Yes, that is very good, you must trust me, Judy.

And you must make up your mind that you are never going to see your sister alive again."

"How can I believe that when you won't swear to me that she's dead?"

"To others I can lie. I am very good at telling lies. But to you . . . I am prevented."

"Then she is—"

"Consider her dead, I tell you!" There was a sudden ferocity in the old man's voice. "And say nothing, nothing, of these feelings and these dreams of yours to anyone but me. It would be very bad for family morale."

"I—know that." Suddenly Judy was on the brink of tears.

He stood over her, a strong tower offering safety, of which now she felt very much in need. "Judy, you must go back to sleep. And you must dream again. Since you have the power of dreams that are so—so vivid, it may be that we can use them. Hear me. Dream not of Kate. Leave Kate to me now. Dream of your brother. Dream of John. Dream . . . "

It seemed to Judy that even as the old man's eyes vanished and his voice ceased, that she was waking up. She was alone in her room, in bed, well tucked beneath her covers, still wearing her robe over her nightgown. Outside the undraped window, the lake-sky showed a dull, gray dawn. Her brother's cries, silent but terrible, were ringing in her mind.

Ten

The phone awoke Joe Keogh from some dark nightmare, the sound an overwhelming relief because it meant nightmares were over and it was time to go to work. He had the receiver in his hand before the memory came that this was supposed to be another day off for him. And why it was.

"Hello Joe, this is Judy."

"Judy—what's up?" It was broad day. His watch, still on his wrist, said after ten. Last night he had drunk too much, finishing a bottle of scotch alone. He didn't notice any hangover, though, just a dullness. All life was a hangover, these days.

Judy's phone voice said: "There's something you have to know."

Now sitting naked on the edge of his single bed, Joe was staring at a curl of house-dust on the bare hardwood floor under the small bedside table that held the phone. That curl had been there when Kate was still alive.

"What is it?" But before he had finished asking, he was sure he knew the answer. Johnny's body had been found.

"Kate's body," the phone-voice told him, and he had a sudden sensation of re-entering a bad dream that he had been through once before. He did not answer immediately.

Judy went on: "She—her—she's missing from the morgue this morning. The Chicago police called us about half an hour ago."

"Missing." Rubbing his eyes made things no clearer. "Are you sure it was really the police who called?" A kidnapping-mutilation and a mysterious death in the same prominent family were sure to draw warped jokers to the scene.

"Yes, the other police are still tapping our phone. And the Chicago police had Dad call them back. It really happened."

Judy's voice sounded more hopeful than dismayed. Well, she was a little weird sometimes. Joe sighed. "It wasn't just some mixup at the morgue? Someone took the wrong body to be buried?"

"It doesn't sound like it could be anything like that. One doctor remembers seeing her there yesterday afternoon. This morning some other doctor went to look, getting ready for the examination. And she was just gone."

He could make no sense of it. "How are you managing, Judy?"

"Mom and Dad are just numb, I think. Gran seems more upset by this than they are."

"Oh. But I meant you."

"Me? I'm coping okay. You sound like you are, too."

"More or less. Look, did you hear from Dr. Corday this morning?"

There was a pause on the line. "Why do you ask? Did he get back to his motel okay last night?"

"Yeah, I dropped him off. Look, just hang in there, kid. I think I'm going to come over and see you."

As Joe hurried into his clothes, his mind was fixed on the remembered face of the old man who last night had been so intent on getting into the morgue. He turned the image from fullface to profile and back again, as if Corday were standing before the black-on-white hatched inchmarks of the lineup. Put on your hat, take it off. No, no face that Joe had ever seen before.

Kate—gone. But that wasn't accurate. Kate had really been gone for days. The body on the right slab or the wrong slab had been hers, but it was not her any longer, and he could feel no vital concern for anything that happened to it. This morning's bad dream wasn't a new tragedy, only a new craziness.

Dressed and shaved, he called the Shores Motel. Dr. Corday was registered there, all right, but his room didn't answer.

Joe decided to give himself time for one cup of instant coffee—after all, there was no way in the world that the old guy could have stolen the body last night, in the five or six or seven minutes he had been out of Joe's sight. Joe dropped two slices of bread into the toaster. Of course, he *could* have returned to the morgue again later . . . .

He sat at the small table in the dining alcove of his small apartment, and tried to get his thinking back into a police track. In police work you couldn't very often accept that strange happenings were just coincidence; last night the rather strange old man had prowled around the morgue, and this morning she was gone.

In police work also, on the other hand, you had to start with what was possible. In fact, the old man could not even have got into the building there last night. Someone had, though—or did Judy have the story garbled?

Still chewing toast, Joe picked up his phone, dialed a number in Homicide, and asked for Charley Snider.

"Charley? This is Joe Keogh. What is it, what's the story?"

"Oh yeah, the story. I'll give it to you straight, man. I know what this must be like for you."

"Just tell me."

"The thing is, she was there as of about ten P.M. last night. Everybody swears all was in order then, at least. Then, man, as of six-ten this A.M., when one of the junior pathologists decides he wants a preliminary look, she was just not there. Empty bin's correctly labeled. All the paper work's in order, as near as we can find out. No bodies were officially removed from the morgue in those eight hours. The only other funny thing is the lockers where the clothes and other personal effects of the, uh, customers are kept; somebody had been digging around in there, it looks like. No locks broken, but the stuff's all scrambled, and we don't know yet if Kate's property is missing or not."

"Family hadn't claimed her things?"

"Not yet they hadn't."

"No signs of a break-in?"

"None we've discovered, it's a big place. We got our men still swarming through there. We're checking out everyone who was on duty there last night. So far's we know, no weirdos among them."

"That's something."

"Hey, man, one more thing. Remember, we found Kate's Lancia in the pound? It had been towed away from that hydrant. Anyway someone left a big fat thumbprint right on the rearview mirror, angle seemed to show it was someone reaching from the right seat. It's being checked out in Washington now."

"It's probably some garage man's. No, it's probably mine; I've ridden in that car a lot."

"If you got any ideas we can try, I'd like to hear."

"No, no ideas." His suspicions of the old man, if they really were suspicions, had to settle into some kind of a sane pattern before he threw them out as a tip. An old friend of Clarissa's, after all. "Thanks, Charley. I'm going over to the Southerlands' for a while, in case you want to reach me."

He sat there for a minute staring at the cradled phone, but seeing the old man. Then he took a jacket from the closet and went out the door.

Snow, gentle-falling, soft as white night, dimmed the scorch of day to muted gray for the old man, dulled for him the multicolored windows of stained glass that in bright sun would have been explosions of discomfort. He needed rest and sleep. Not, as yet, to the point where his

survival was in question, so he stayed on his feet
and active. Tomorrow, though, he was certainly
going to have to sleep.

Besides dulling the sun, another eminently
satisfactory effect of the snow was that it seemed
to discourage visitors to Lockwood Cemetery. Or
perhaps Americans were just not as enthusiastic
as Europeans about visiting their dead. Anyway,
during the whole morning he had heard no more
than three or four vehicles whispering around the
gravel roads of the cemetery, one of them a pick-
up truck with snowplow attached, that seemed to
make but little progress in getting the drives clear.

Gently, but very insistantly, the snow continued to fall. By two o'clock it lay ankle-deep on the
broad lawns and weathered stones of the cemetery's old section, and clung to the wrought-iron
fences, obscuring the signs that warned about the
guard dogs being loosed here after dusk. The
snow and the dogs were all fine with the old man
who stood looking out from inside the Southerland mausoleum, his eye to a small chink he had
broken in one window of stained glass.

He supposed that this mausoleum was old and
large, as such things went in this young country.
It was a one-room house of marble no warmer and
no colder than the snow, or than the bones it
sheltered—or than the living but unbreathing
flesh that it concealed today.

At intervals, when he grew weary of looking
out, five or six long paces took the old man from
one end of the cold room to the other. This in-
cluded a slight detour around the empty sarcophagus and the decorative urns that had been

planted in the middle of the space. Looking at them, he could see why Andrew had exiled them here, ugly decorations no one wanted to behold. The central sarcophagus was unoccupied; so far all interments had been in the vaults built into the thick outer walls. Southerlands and their kin who had died in the past seventy years or so were there, behind waist-high doors of green-patinaed bronze.

Kate was lying just above one such door, on a wide marble ledge set below another stained-glass window. She had been lying there since just before the wintry dawn, curled up like a sleeper, wrapped in a sheet that revealed only her head.

Kate lay on her left side, facing the room, but with eyes closed. One arm tucked beneath her head, she had scarcely moved for hours. The coarse sheet wrapping her from toes to neck bore on one corner the stamped legend, PROPERTY OF COOK COUNTY MEDICAL EXAMINER'S OFFICE. While she was not fully awake, she was not fully asleep either; which was one reason why the old man, finding himself thrust into the role of midwife for her new life, hesitated to leave her alone, even though other important matters demanded his attention.

This half-sleeping condition of Kate's had him somewhat puzzled. No reason, he thought, why she should not be able to sleep the daylight hours away, in this her native sepulcher. In fact when he brought her here he had expected her to slip into a deep sleep at once.

He came back now from another squint out of the broken window, to stand motionlessly regard-

ing her. His black topcoat was open, his dark hat
set at a slightly jaunty angle, his dark glasses off,
his hands behind his back.

Suddenly Kate's eyes flew open. "I don't know
you," she said, in dazed mistrustfulness. Her
speech was newly awkward: sometimes she forgot to take a breath before she started talking, for
breath was no longer a requirement of her life;
sometimes she drew in too much air, and the end
of a phrase was punctuated with a sharp puff of
the surplus.

She had protested that he was a stranger
enough times for him to have lost count. But if
patience with her confusion was costing him an
effort, he had not let that effort show as yet. "I am
an old friend of the family, Kate," he repeated, yet
again. "Of your Grandmother Clarissa's in particular. I have brought you here for your own
protection."

Kate moved her body substantially now for the
first time in hours, rising on one elbow. "*How* did
you bring me here?"

This question and answer too, they had been
through several times before. "Think back,
girl—what do you remember of our journey?"

Kate's blue eyes looked into the distance. This
time round she was going to manage to take the
conversation at least one step farther than before.
"There were doors, somewhere . . . in a couple of
different places . . . and you told me that because
it was after dark we needed no keys; we could slip
through."

"What else?"

"It seems to me that I can remember—flying.
Like something in a dream."

"Trust your memory, Kate. It was no dream.

Now, what is the last thing that you can recall *before* our journey? Think carefully."

Obediently she retired into her own thoughts, to surface again in a few moments. "I can remember being at a party."

"Excellent! We are making progress. Where was the party?"

"I . . . can't remember."

"Try."

Kate seemed to be trying, but had no success. He pressed on: "After the party, then. You perhaps left with someone?"

"Yes . . ."

"Who was it?" The old man could hear, perhaps half a kilometer away, the snowplow scraping slowly.

"He said . . ." Suddenly Kate sat bolt upright on her shelf, clutching the sheet about her. "He said his name was Enoch Winter."

"You have said that name before." The questioner nodded with satisfaction. "And what does Enoch Winter look like, little one?"

"He's big. Very tall. Very strong." The last word ended with a little shudder, wherein horror and repulsion were mingled with the memory of delight.

"Taller than I am? Look at me."

Obediently Kate looked. "Oh, yes. By several inches."

For a long time, he mused, I was considered very tall myself Now I am scarcely above the average, I suppose. Shall I someday qualify as a midget?

Aloud, he asked: "His hair? His eyes? His face?"

"Dark curly hair. Sort of a deep voice, but much

rougher than yours. His eyes are blue, or maybe gray. I'll know him if I see him again."

"Indeed, I should think you—" He broke off, watching her with great intentness.

Kate's gradual return to full awareness had reached a critical point. Now she was looking with terror at the marble walls, the stained glass, and the tombs surrounding her. "What is this place?" Her breath momentarily forgotten, the question fell into a mere soundless mouthing of the words. Then she drew in a gasp of air. "I know where I am. I know what this is."

"I am your friend," the old man said with iron will, "and you are safe."

Words, even from him, were not going to be enough. Kate screamed and leaped in mad panic from her shelf, a corner of the sheet trailing like a cape. She landed awkwardly, but with catlike new strength supporting unsprained ankles. Without a pause she sprang toward the single door of the mausoleum.

Before she reached it, though, the old man was beside her, and had an arm around her waist. Despite the new strength with which she struggled, he drew her back and soothed her like a child. "No, no. You do not understand the dangers yet."

A moment longer Kate fought for her freedom. Then she slumped in his grip, her eyes crazed. "I want to go home."

His clasp was almost tender. "I think you know," he said, "that you are as close to home right now as you are ever likely to get."

A few seconds passed. This time the movement she made to free herself was deliberate and almost calm, and so he released her. She moved a few steps off and turned to face him, now fully aware—and horrified. "I heard a policeman say that I was dead."

"Very likely you did."

"You can't convince me that I'm dead!"

"My dear girl, I have no intention of trying to convince you of such an absurdity. Neither of us is dead—except to our old, breathing lives."

"Then—what—?"

"You have been through a great change. And understanding it is going to take some time." Acceptance and understanding, the old man knew, did not often come fully on the first day out of the grave.

Kate was frowning down at her swathing sheet. "Where are my clothes?"

The old man walked to one of the crypts and tugged open its bronze door. The interior was empty save for two bags, one a white laundry sack, the other somewhat smaller, and elegant black. He brought both of them back to Kate. "You have some choice of apparel, though I am not sure the outfit in the white bag is complete."

Wonderingly, Kate reached into the laundry sack and extracted from it first her warm blue jacket, rolled up small; then blue pants and a sweater. She looked at the old man with narrowed eyes, then dug into the other bag. Out first came brown slacks, then a brown sweater, shoes to match, a small mass of soft undergarments. "These are mine." There was more sharpness than fear in her voice now. "But I was wearing the blue. Where did you get these?"

"Ah, memory is firming up. Good. The brown

clothing I obtained very early this morning, from your home."

"My home. You've been there. What did you tell them, what—?"

"Gently, Kate, gently. Your family thinks that you are dead."

She shook her head. She backed away from the old man a step, her lips forming another word.

"He thinks so, too. For the time being, at least, it is better so. Later, there will be decisions you must make, regarding those you love. But that must come later, when you know more. Now I am going to look out the window while you dress. Then will we discuss what must be done."

When he turned from squinting at the snow, he found Kate garbed in brown. He took from her the blue clothing, including the warm jacket she no longer needed. These garments he put back into the empty crypt, the only convenient drawer this dwelling-place afforded.

Challengingly, Kate followed him. He smiled to see in her something of her younger sister's bravery. "Now," she demanded, "I want to know who you are, really. And what has really happened to me."

"Very well." He looked steadily into her eyes. "I am a vampire, Kate. Because Enoch Winter exchanged his vampire blood with you, you have become a vampire also. I am sure that there is in your mind much superstitious nonsense regarding our race, which you must now begin to unlearn. We are not all as bad as Enoch Winter."

The girl first tried to laugh at him. Then she tried to look indignant, that he should offer her such nonsense. He could see her wondering what

she should try next. He could see also that the
energy of terror was fading; a normal daylight
trance should overcome her soon.

"But why," the old man mused aloud, "has the
infamous Enoch Winter done this? Under other
circumstances we might merely ask why any
rapist does what he does. But there is also the
attack on your brother to be considered. There
must surely be a connection."

"What attack?" Kate didn't completely believe,
yet, anything he'd said. But already she was swaying on her feet.

"Time to discuss that later." He picked her up,
gently; it was almost a matter of catching her as
she began to fall. One of her pale hands pushed
feebly at his chest in protest, but her eyelids were
closing, and she could do no more.

Now she should sleep, until the night at least.
But before he put her in a resting place, he stood
for a moment, listening intently. A motor vehicle,
a small auto whose sound he thought he might
just possibly recognize, was drawing near over
the cemetery's unplowed drives.

Joe Keogh's Rabbit crunched to a stop in snow
unmarked except for a few tracks left by the fur-
bearing variety. He supposed the bunnies had a
good thing going in a cemetery, except maybe
after hours when the guard dogs were let in.
Anyway the snowfall had now stopped, though
the sky was still almost completely overcast. In
the west the clouds were stretched to a thin silver
sheet covering a sun already on its way to the
horizon. The shortest days of the year were here.

Beside Joe, Judy sat gazing with an unreadable

expression at the snow-etched stones of the mausoleum's front. He studied her with concern for a little while, then asked: "Did you want to look at something in particular?"

Still looking at the building, Judy shook her head slowly, disappointedly, almost. What could she have been expecting? She said: "It's just that the dreams were very real."

"But still only dreams," he told her gently. "Right?"

She didn't answer.

"Get a hold of yourself, kid. How could they be anything else? Kate is dead. Whatever else has . . . I admit it's possible that Johnny might be locked up in a closet someplace, the way you describe it in your dream. But—"

"Joe, I could find that place. I know I could, if you would only drive me around and help me look."

"Don't start that again, please." And at that moment, beyond Judy's face, beyond the undisturbed white that covered lawn and walk in front of the Southerland mausoleum, Joe saw the green-aged bronze of the building's door in motion, opening inward into a contrasting blackness. And despite the hardened realism created by eight years on the force, the sight produced a moment when something in his heart began to open into blackness also.

Then it was nothing more frightening than a shadowed doorway in a marble building, with the recognized though unexpected figure of a lean man in dark clothing emerging from it in a quite ordinary way. A penetrating voice called down to them: "Judy? Joe?"

Judy, Joe noticed, seemed not at all surprised. Perhaps she was no longer disappointed, either. Frowning, he shut off the engine. They both got out of the car.

Corday had remained beside the mausoleum's open door, frowning through dark glasses at his watch. "I fear I have lost all track of time," he muttered as Judy and Joe trudged up the virgin walk toward him. "The urns proved more engrossing than I had anticipated."

"My father did give you the key, then," Judy remarked placidly, twirling the end of her scarf. Joe wondered suddenly: could she have been expecting that we'd meet him here?

Corday was smiling at her lightly. "There was no trouble about the key."

Joe asked him: "How did you get out here, Doctor? Take a cab?"

"No, someone kindly offered me a ride from the motel this morning."

"Must've been early. Snow's covered all the tracks completely."

"Indeed, it was."

Judy put in: "If you're ready to leave, we can take you back to the motel. Or wherever you want to go."

"Thank you, my dear, that would be kind."

Corday was in the act of pulling the mausoleum door shut behind him when Joe stepped forward, saying: "As long as we're here, I'd like to take a look at the pottery too . . . Judy, what's wrong?"

"Nothing. I just felt a little dizzy, all of a sudden. I'm all right. You go on in, but I don't want to."

She looked so white-faced that Joe and Corday

between them, both peering at her anxiously, walked her down to the car and saw her settled in the rear seat.

"I feel better now. I think it was just a little too much like the dream. Go ahead, Joe, I'm all right."

The two men marched back up to the dark doorway, over the now well-trampled walk.

"You first, Doctor."

With a slight bow, the old man went on in. Joe followed. Once inside, there was really plenty of light, coming in the windows. The doorway had looked so black from outside only by contrast with the snow.

Plenty of light, but not all that much to see. Joe wasn't really sure what he was looking for. The tombs and their decorations, and the big urns, and maybe Corday was really enthusiast enough to want to spend a day here in the cold among them. Joe's breath steamed in the air. To him, the place looked not much different from a fancier-than-usual funeral home, or the inside of one of the older Chicago churches. It reminded him a little of the chapel of Thomas More University, where he had been going to take Kate a couple of days before Christmas, to see *The Play of Daniel* . . . there was plenty of pottery here, all right, and in this large urn someone's crumpled bra, which must have been here since last summer, so evidently the door wasn't always kept carefully locked.

As soon as his eyes met Corday's again, he told the old man bluntly: "Kate's body was missing from the morgue this morning."

Corday's response was controlled surprise, or at

least a very good imitation thereof. "Really? Is such a thing a common occurrence there?"

"Very uncommon. I was wondering if you might have any ideas about it."

"Because I wanted to go there last night? No. No, I should not care to venture an opinion. Joe, what brings you and Judy here to the cemetery this afternoon?"

Joe sighed. "The kid had a very vivid dream last night. A couple of dreams, rather. She's upset—of course. Anyway, one dream was that Kate was here, in the family mausoleum, alive, but unable to get out of the place for some reason. And all day today Judy's been saying she thought she'd go crazy if she couldn't get out of the house for a while. Andy's back at the office, being a workaholic as usual. Lenore is—sedated. Clarissa can't decide anything. I finally just took it upon myself to decide that Judy would be better off getting out, and it'd be safe enough if I rode shotgun." He blinked at Corday's blank stare. "Chicago cops always go armed, you know, even off duty. So here we are."

While Joe talked they had been slowly gravitating back to the doorway. Now Corday gestured and Joe stepped out. At the bottom of the little slope, Judy's scarf-wreathed face smiled back from the small car's window.

Joe led the way down to her. Behind him he could hear Corday shutting the metal door of the mausoleum carefully, and the key turning, grating, in the little-used lock.

Judy looked well enough when they rejoined her in the car. "I think it was just the idea of going in there," she said again. "I didn't want to go in after all."

"Natural enough," said Joe, getting the engine and heater started. *Why was the old man here, today?* "Where can we take you, Dr. Corday?"

The old man, in the right front seat, was twisting round to face the back. "Joe tells me you had two vivid dreams last night. What was the second?"

Judy smiled, a quick little flicker, as if to mark the passage of some secret between her and the old man. Then her face turned bleak. "Towards morning I dreamed of Johnny. He was in a closet somewhere. All naked, and bloody, and . . . just awful. God, I hope it isn't true. But I can't stop feeling that it is."

"And can you lead us to this closet?" The old man was intensely serious.

"I'm taking her home," said Joe, and reached to move his selector lever into Drive. The old man's fingers settled gently on his wrist. Joe urged his own hand forward anyway; his hand stayed right where it was, as if he were trying to lift the car with it instead of one thin elderly arm. He felt ridiculous. What was he going to do now, start a wrestling match?

The old man continued to stare at Judy, and Joe followed the direction of his gaze. He was disturbed to see that although Judy still sat up straight, her eyes were closed and the utterly relaxed expression on her face suggested that she was asleep.

In wonder, he asked: "Judy?"

"She is asleep," Corday informed him soothingly, and at the same time let go of [...]e's wrist.

"Judy, are you all right?"

"Answer Joe, Judy."

"I'm fine." Her voice was pleasant, bu[...]
Her eyes stayed closed.

Corday asked her: "Can you now guide us [...]te.
building where John is being held?"

"Yes." Her voice held sudden urgency. "[...]
west as soon as you leave the cemetery."

Joe looked at her a moment longer, then got the
car in motion, this time without interference.
"What is she, hypnotized? Whatever you're doing
with her, I don't like it. She's going home."

"Joe, don't." Judy's voice was intense but calm.
"I'm all right. If you love Kate, you'll help to find
her brother."

Joe glanced into the rear-view mirror. Judy's
eyes were open again and she looked quite normal.

She said: "Do you think the police are ever
going to find him? They don't have a single real
clue, do they?"

They had reached the plowed section of the
cemetery roads by now. The gate was only a quarter mile or so ahead. Joe said: "If you want the
truth, I don't think they'll ever get him back
alive."

"There you are. But we can. He's in a white
house, out in the country just a few miles west of
here. I think the roof has shingles."

"I think you better go home."

"If you try to take me home I'll jump out of the
car before we get there. I'll fight and scream. If you
humor me a little I'll be just fine."

d, indecisively. Half angry, half plead-

Joe slp, he turned to the old man. "Doctor?"

ing by's face was altered by a smile, small,
ent, and almost irresistibly comradely.
y he said: "Turn west."

Eleven

"Your hour's almost up," Joe commented. Almost an hour after leaving Lockwood Cemetery, they had at last penetrated the western belt of suburbs and were entering real countryside. The two-lane highway, coated in salted slush, ran northwest. On the left were cornfields, snowy stubble now, and on the right at the moment was a new apartment development, decorated barracks that seemed to have been extruded against the road's shoulder by the congestion to the east.

"Keep going," Judy urged. Again, as happened every time Joe so much as hinted at giving up, there was an underlevel of panic in her reply. "Joe, he's so badly hurt. We've got to get to him right away. There's a man in the house with Johnny, but he's not helping Johnny at all. I can *feel* how close it is. We're almost there."

"Six more minutes," said Joe firmly. "Then we're going to find a phone and call your home and tell 'em you're all right. I agreed to spend an hour at this, and we will, and then you're going home. Right, Doctor?"

No answer came from Corday, who had his hands in his coat pockets, and was gazing fixedly ahead, as if he were lost in his own thoughts.

Joe did not repeat the question. There had been moments during the ride when mentally he swore at himself for being taken in by Judy's hysterics and Corday's strange act, and came very close to turning the car around at once. These moments were followed by others in which he nursed the feeling, hardly suitable for a cop but inextinguishable anyway, that weird things in the field of ESP did sometimes happen. His own mother and father had testified to mutual experiences. And the rational part of his mind suggested that the best way to cure Judy of this dream-idea might be to let her see that there was nothing in it. And, again, to get a kidnapping victim back, any effort at all was worth a try.

They were approaching a highway intersection. "What do I do here?" he asked his guide.

"Turn left," Judy ordered. Give her credit, she was always decisive in giving directions. "We're very close now. Another mile should do it."

"Left it is," Joe agreed. He could just picture himself talking to the sheriff's office on the phone: Yessir, we know where the boy is now. His teenage sister saw it in a dream, and sure enough . . .

The new highway ran ahead of him almost straight, and almost empty. The sun, after almost breaking through the clouds a little earlier, had been smothered again in thick gray masses from which it did not seem likely to emerge again today. Although theoretically it was still daylight, Joe had already flicked his headlights on.

The last housing developments had now fallen behind. To right and left the road was bordered by snowy farm fields, brown hedgerows, patches of woods, wire farm fences. A narrow highway bridge came leaping up to bear the Volkswagen over a still narrower stream, a country creek that twisted its way in a frozen course to right and left. For just a moment the engine stuttered—

"Here!" The word burst out of Judy in a shriek. Joe looked wildly around for some impending accident. He braked, avoiding a skid in the freezing slush by fancy footwork on the pedals.

Judy's fingers were biting like claws at his shoulder. "That next drive on our left," she agonized. "Take that, he's in a house back there."

Joe had brought the small car to a complete stop on the shoulder of the highway. Now he eased it forward. Looking ahead on the left, he could now see that there was a driveway, a small unpaved road, a something, and he turned into it, between patches of hedgerow. A rural mailbox planted beside the highway was capped with snow, making any name that it might bear invisible.

Trackless snow also covered the narrow lane or drive. But the surface beneath was evidently solid and level, for going was not difficult. Almost at the start the drive turned, taking them out of sight of the highway among wintry thickets and small trees. It ran straight for fifty yards or so, then turned again, at the same time topping a small rise of ground.

Just before reaching this second turn, Joe eased the Rabbit to a stop. Directly ahead there had just come into his view the upper portion of one end of what he would later learn was a sprawling, white brick, ranch-style house. Now, squinting into the dusk, he thought he could make out cedar roof-shingles under a partial covering of snow.

Oddly, Joe felt almost cheated. He looked at the calm, unreadable face beside him for several seconds before he spoke. "I don't know what this game is, mister."

Corday's thin lips parted, this time not in a smile. "It is a very serious game indeed. And I assure you that you and I are playing it on the same side." Peering toward the house, the old man added, as if to himself: "The sun has not yet set."

"What's that got to do with anything?"

Judy said in a tight voice: "Do something, please, Joe. You're a policeman. My brother is in there."

Joe looked at them both. Then he put the car in reverse and backed it up a few yards, getting it completely out of sight of the house. He turned the ignition off. He looked at them both again, and shook his head. "Judy, you know I've got no authority, outside the city. I'll do this much: walk up to the front door and see who's home, if anyone. You two stay here, just sit tight."

Judy started to demand that he do more than that, but Corday reached back to touch her wrist and she fell silent. Joe got out of the car and, with a last look at Corday, took the keys with him. "Be back in a minute or so."

Readying a story about car trouble and needing to use a phone, he trudged the last yards toward the house, following the curve of the drive through completely untracked snow. It was all crazy, of course. Somehow Judy must have glimpsed from the highway a white house and a shingle roof . . .

The only sign of life that Joe could see ahead was the subtle wavering of heated air above a chimney. Not the great brick one that would have a fireplace at its base, but the small metal tube that would vent the house's furnace to the air. The furnace was turned on, then. But the garage door and the front door under its shingled overhang were both sealed along their bases with unbroken snow. No light showed in any window. There were no Christmas decorations, either, if that meant anything, which it probably did not.

When he reached the front door he alternately pushed the bell button and knocked, police style, keeping up a steady barrage in a way that almost always got results, making whoever was inside think that there was some real emergency. The doorbell worked, for he could faintly hear the chime. It wasn't answered, though.

A full minute of such thorough treatment got no results. Joe tried to peer into a large window on the porch beside the door, but the drapes were too tightly shut inside. Not quite ready to give up yet, he started around the house, looking for tracks or other signs of occupancy, and finding nothing that seemed consequential. A couple of imperfectly draped windows let him peek into a couple of rooms, which were empty of furniture. He did see some new-looking paint and shiny floors, as if some remodeling or refinishing project might recently have been completed; but it was too dark inside to be sure of even that much. It might be that the owners had moved out during the remodeling, but had left the heat turned on to protect the water pipes and the new plaster.

His circuit of the house completed, Joe approached the front step again, thinking: one more knock, so I can say I really tried. When we get back to the highway, I'll check the name on that mailbox—just to be thorough.

Fiercely Judy hissed the words, almost in the ear of the old man who sat in the seat ahead: "He is in that house!"

"I do not doubt that, Judy." Lean fingers on the door handle beside him, the old man was staring ahead with serpent-like intensity. "But neither do I think that Joe is going to discover him. He is an honorable policeman, who will not dream of exceeding his authority on grounds no stronger than those which we have given him."

"We can't go away and leave Johnny in there!"

"We certainly cannot. Especially since this visit must alarm his captor. You say you see only one man with him, now?"

"Yes."

"I think you are right." And with the movement of a lithe twenty-year-old, Corday was suddenly out of the car. He held the door open, his tall form bending beside it, looking in at her. "I am going to take action. And you . . . but no."

"What is it?" She had never seen eyes like his . . . they were so dark. And they were old no longer.

He said, eyes glittering: "I was about to order you to stay here in safety. But this is not the world for safety, is it? Nor are you and I the people who prize it above all. So, will you enter battle with me? In all the world are very few whom I would sooner ask."

The man who spoke to her seemed to have been transformed, to have grown larger than life. And it seemed to Judy that she was transformed too. The young woman who stepped out of the car was a fit companion for heroic deeds. Yet she was still herself, perhaps more truly herself than ever before.

"What must I do?" she calmly asked.

"Come this way at once. Joe is returning." Her companion's voice had altered too, and there were hints of drums and trumpets even in its softness.

She followed him as quickly as she could, along the edge of the drive back in the direction of the highway.

"Now jump this way," he ordered. "Leave no tracks." The best spring of her young legs took her sideways from the drive, to an area of matted leaves and brown grass that had been blown free of snow. From one snowless patch to the next she followed her companion, who moved ahead now like an acrobat, reaching back a hand from time to time to steady her. He led her through grass and bush and briefly along the top rail of a split-log fence, in a curving path that brought them into some bushes from which they could just see the car.

Crouching there motionless, with Corday's hand upon her arm, Judy could see the alarm in Joe's face as he came trotting the last yards to the vehicle, shocked by the realization that they were gone. "Corday?" he called out, almost threateningly. Then, louder: "Judy!"

In a moment he had spotted their footprints in the snow, leading back along the drive. Swearing, he started after them on foot, and promptly lost the trail where the snow gave way in spots to leaves and grass. Red-faced and muttering, Joe jumped into the car. Spinning wheels in snow, he got the Volks turned round and headed back to the highway. The sound of it died away.

"Now, my girl." Corday—this youthful stranger she had known as Corday—stood up straight, raising her by both arms to stand beside him. "Before I can enter any house, I must be called, invited, by someone inside. Do not ask me to explain just now, but it is so. So you must get into this house, somehow, and then call to me. If no one answers the door for you, break in a window."

"I will." Around Judy the woods were growing minute by minute dimmer, darkness oozing up into them from the ground. But for the moment she was not at all afraid.

"Only call me, and I shall come. But you must call."

Life sang in Judy's blood, life of an intensity that nothing in her memory could match. It forced her to a knowledge that she had earlier refused. She breathed: "I called you once before. Didn't I?"

The man before her nodded quickly, his timeless eyes joyful that she understood. "But ask no questions now," he said. With a light pressure of his hand he sent her on her way.

Fear did not begin until she was out of the woods and well along the drive toward the house, where all the windows were utterly dark in the swiftly gathering twilight. The snow under Judy's booted feet was marked now with Joe's tracks, going and returning. And now she could see where someone, probably Joe also, had circled the house.

On the raised step under the protective overhang of roof that sheltered the front door, the snow was not as deep as in the open yard. It was much trampled by Joe's feet, but an unbroken white grommet remaining between door and threshold showed that the door had not been opened for him. Judy rang the doorbell at once, heard the faint chime, and only then wondered what she would say if someone came. Her car had broken down, that would be it.

But no one answered.

A quick glance to her rear showed only the darkening gloom of woods and lawn and fields, but she knew Corday was there. Before her, she could still feel the habitation of the house. But there was no sound or light to give corroboration to the feeling.

She knocked, then rang again. Inside, she felt—she knew—that Johnny heard the bell. Johnny, locked up in fear and pain and darkness, unable or afraid to even cry out.

The window beside the front door, Judy soon discovered, could not be opened from the outside. Not by her pulling or pushing at it, at least. She balled a fist inside her mitten, then paused long enough to take off her scarf and wrap it round her hand.

Judy's first blow at the glass was not wholehearted enough to break it in, and she gave a little cry of frustration before she punched again. This time there was a satisfactory crash, followed by a tinkle on the floor inside.

As if the crash had been a signal prearranged, the front door was suddenly thrown wide. A young man, thick-necked and muscular but rather small, stood there wearing faded jeans and an old army shirt. One hand was out of sight on each side of the door frame. His neatly trimmed hair was somehow incongruous. His eyes were partially hidden behind the distortion of thick glasses; his mouth, twisted in rage or fear or both, was open on uneven teeth.

"What're you doing?" The man's voice was breathless, almost unintelligible with apparent strain.

Its urgent menace for the moment made Judy forget everything else and she took an involuntary step backward. "I—I need help with my car."

"For that you break the window? Who was that guy who was just here?"

"I . . ." From some inward source, invention came. "I asked a man to help me. Now I don't know where he's gone."

"No help here. There's a gas station down the highway, east, about half a mile." The man's extreme excitement had perhaps eased just a little. He had not changed his position in the doorway yet.

"I don't think I can walk that far," Judy pleaded. "Please, let me use your phone."

"Get outta here," he muttered, almost as if his thoughts were already on something else. He kept darting glances past her into the snowy dusk.

Judy was mastering her fright. Her nerves still vibrated in sympathy with her brother's unceasing pain. "I won't go away," she said, regaining her lost step toward the door. "I can't."

The young man looked at her with very ugly eyes.

She faced his look. "I'm just going to stand here and scream until you let me in."

Her desperation though not the reason for it, evidently impressed itself upon him. Several things, most of them frightening, passed through the young man's face in quick succession. Finally caution in some form prevailed.

"All right, I'll come take a look at your goddamned car," he muttered. "Breaking the goddamned window—" He turned away as if meaning to grab a coat from somewhere close at hand. As he retreated he pushed the door from inside, shutting it almost completely.

Not giving herself time to think, Judy sprang forward, throwing her body against the closing door. It burst open before her rush. "Johnny!" she screamed.

A ceiling light just inside the entry had now been switched on. The rest of the house, as far as she could tell, was all in darkness. The floor of the large entryway was tiled, and on the opposite side of it the young man stood before an open closet door. Not the closet that she wanted, no. He was in the act of pulling on a bulky sheepskin jacket, and in his free hand there dangled a long-barreled, very real-looking revolver. His face was just now turning toward Judy in fresh astonishment.

To Judy's left, a great living room, devoid of

furniture but thickly carpeted, stretched to a distant red-brick fireplace wall. Somewhere in that direction, a little farther off, Johnny was cowering in his prison, chained and gagged by fear, radiating pain like heat from glowing metal. Judy's screaming of his name still rang like a distant alarm in his dazed brain, and from there back to her own mind again.

"Johnny!" she cried again. "I'm here!" And she moved toward the living room, to place herself between her helpless brother and this armed maniac.

The young man in the sheepskin stepped across the entry and slammed the front door closed again. His face was evilly contorted now. Without a word he moved toward Judy, the weapon in his hand rising with what seemed like endless slowness.

At last remembering what she was supposed to do, Judy cried out: "Come in, Dr. Corday, help me!" As she cried she ducked away from her attacker, to find herself falling softly down the single step from entryway to sunken living room. Her arms were raised to protect her head from blows or bullets. Her last glimpse of the young man as she turned away showed him reaching toward her with his left hand.

Even as the house spun with her spinning fall, she heard the front door fly open with a violent crash. There was a roaring of cold air in the room, an incomprehensible sudden wind that had blasted open the closed door. The hand that had just brushed Judy's arm fell away. Then the door slammed shut again with a thunderous bang.

The wind gave one last, trailing howl, and disappeared.

The house was quiet.

Judy raised her face from the thick carpet and sat up. Corday was in the act of crouching down beside her, one hand outstretched. His fingers touched her hair. "Judy, it is all right now. You are not hurt?"

She jumped to her feet. "Find Johnny."

Her companion was already in motion, his long strides carrying him off into the darkness engulfing the rear portion of the house.

Before following, Judy looked around. The front door was tightly closed once more, though now a portion of its lock hung in at an angle among splinters of newly broken wood. On the other side of the living room, near the great fireplace, the young man's sheepskin coat lay in a bulky mound, and near it the long-barreled revolver. He must have run outside. . . .

"Judy?" Corday's penetrating voice reached her from some distant room. "He is in here."

She ran down a dark hallway, past dim, unfurnished bedrooms, and a bathroom where she could make out a dirty towel hung on a rack, soap in a grimy puddle on a lavatory top. Light shone out of another bedroom, where Corday was waiting for her. A small lamp burned on an upended crate that served as bedside table for an unmade cot. Odds and ends of men's clothes were strewn about, along with girly magazines, weightlifting journals, bits of food and garbage, tin cans, paper cups, plates, a small transistor radio.

Corday stood beside the open door of the huge

closet, gesturing for Judy to go in ahead of him. "He looks bad," he said with his usual calm. "But I believe he will recover."

No clothes were hanging in the closet. Inside, Judy dropped to her knees beside the horrible, pale figure contracted into one dim corner. The figure stirred, raising a head matted with long, dirt-colored hair. Against its naked chest were folded two mummified Egyptian hands, covered with dried brownish stains, their fingers clenched and twisted.

Startlingly pale eyes appeared, in a face that might once have been her brother's. "Judy," a stranger's voice croaked at her. "They caught you, too."

"No, oh no. Oh, Johnny, your poor hands."

Corday was in and out of the closet now, moving with impersonal gentleness and quite improbable speed. He helped Johnny stand, looked at his throat closely for some reason, then wrapped him in two blankets from the cot. Somehow he found Johnny's own boots and helped Judy get them on his feet. There seemed, for some reason, to be a tremendous hurry.

"You are to drive him directly home, Judy, stopping for nothing, except to avoid a collision."

"The car—"

"There is a car in the garage, and unless I am mistaken these are its keys." He handed her a jingling ring. "Hurry ahead and get the engine started—down the hall to your right. I shall bring John."

In grabbing for the keys Judy accidentally bumped her brother's arm and he cried out in pain. Then she flew down the hall in the direction

Corday had indicated. She caught a last glimpse of the living room in passing; the bundle of sheepskin coat had legs, she saw from this angle, and it was stirring now, raising a face.

A light was on already in the garage, and its door had been rolled up. She was already behind the wheel of the Cadillac, engine started and headlights on, as Corday arrived to stow her brother in beside her.

"Shouldn't we telephone someone first—"

"Joe will be calling for help. Drive straight home now, stop for nothing. Leave all else to me."

"Judy?" The voice coming from the pale face beside her did sound a little like her brother's now, though terribly weak. "Take me home now?"

Corday had already slammed the Cadillac's door shut and vanished back into the house. Even as Judy gunned the engine and pulled out of the garage, two muffled banging noises from in there reached her ears. She had driven miles toward home before it occurred to her excited mind that they might possibly have been shots.

Twelve

Of the two uniformed Cook County sheriff's deputies who had met Joe at the country gas station in response to his phone call, and had then followed him back to this lonely house, one was now outside in their official car, busy with its radio. The other deputy was with Joe in the house, and had begun a more or less methodical questioning of the only other person who had been on the scene when they arrived.

"Now, you say he fired twice at you, Dr. Corday? Where were you standing when that happened?"

"I believe—here." And Corday moved decisively to a position in the living room not far from the entry. He seemed to have been not in the least shaken by the peril through which, according to his own story, he had so recently passed.

"Uhuh." The deputy remarked. He was not especially excited either. Following the old man closely he pointed to, without quite touching, a shattery-looking place in the otherwise new-looking plaster wall behind him. "If that is a bullet hole, I guess you weren't standing *exactly* where you are right now, when she hit."

"Approximately," Corday conceded, turning to look with mild interest at the damage.

The deputy made a note. "You say he fired twice . . . one could be in the carpet somewhere, I suppose."

"That seems not improbable. As I recall, his arm was shaking."

"Then he ran out of the house, you say. Did you make any attempt to hold him?"

"I am not as young as I once was, officer."

"Yessir, I don't blame you a bit for that. Don't get me wrong. But first, he did let you load the kidnap victim into a car and drive him out of here? I don't quite understand that."

Corday blinked mildly at the deputy. "Perhaps the young man, even though he had a gun, was frightened when Miss Southerland and I broke in."

"Perhaps. Huh. You say you're the one who broke the door in? How'd you manage that?"

"Construction standards are not what they were in the old days."

"Well, that's for sure." Scratching his head, the deputy gave Joe a wary look: You know this old guy, huh? You didn't warn me he was a little crazy.

Corday added: "And it is not always the brave, is it, who bear weapons?"

"That's for *damn* sure." The deputy sighed. "Now, sir, tell me again—how'd you know the

Southerland boy was here, as you say he was?"

"I repeat, I am an accomplished hypnotist—"
The old man broke off, turning to watch the front
door. A few seconds later it grated open. This time
a piece of the smashed lock fell completely free.

Deputy Two, wide-eyed, stopped in the doorway. "Carl! I just got the Glenlake chief on the
horn. He confirms what our witness here says.
Both the Southerland kids are home, they drove
up a few minutes ago in someone's Caddy. The
girl says they came from out here. The boy has the
little finger missing from each hand. They're taking him to Evanston Hospital. The FBI and
everyone else is gonna be out here on our ass in
about ten minutes."

"Jesus," said Deputy One, with fervor. He gave
the old man a look that showed how little of the
old man's story had been believed, up until this
moment. "Well, let's not screw up anything until
they get here."

"Carl, I'm gonna take a look around outside.
The suspect is supposed to have run out, isn't
he?"

Number One considered. "Right. I guess you
better. But don't screw up anything. Don't mess
up the tracks in the snow, if there are any. I guess
there must be, if the guy ran out."

"I'll come along," Joe volunteered. "I can show
you which tracks are mine, at least."

"Thanks, that would be a help."

Outside, more snow was now falling, in the
form of frigidly dry powder. From the front step,
Deputy Two's powerful flashlight swept the yard.
"The longer we wait, the harder it's gonna be to
find anything."

"Those tracks going all the way around the house are mine," Joe pointed out. "Now there, those are new." From the front step a narrow, fresh trail led in a straight diagonal across the yard, angling away from the drive.

"I'd say *two* people."

"Not side by side, though. One following the other."

"Or chasing the other, maybe."

They started across the yard themselves, keeping parallel with the trail they followed. The deputy led with his flash, Joe stepping into the deputy's tracks.

Joe said: "I think they were both running."

"Jesus, I think you're right. Look, can this be one stride, from here to here? It must be ten feet long."

"I'm no expert at this tracking bit."

"Hell, I'm not either."

At the edge of the yard the makers of the double trail had somehow negotiated a decorative, split-rail fence. On the other side of the fence the trail went on, still practically in a straight line, through a patch of young woods and down an easy slope.

Following the deputy over the fence and on, Joe muttered: "Couldn't have been running to get to a road this way, could they? Highways back in the other direction."

"All that's down this way is the creek, I think—hey."

A few yards ahead, the slope flattened into what would be in summer muddy creek-bottom land. The dead stalks of last summer's growth of weeds made a thin, wintry jungle, more than head-high

but fragile and offering no real impediment to
progress. Along the trail a number of the dried
stalks had been broken down in its direction. Not
many yards farther on, the flashlight's beam now
reached the frozen creek itself, a sunken aisle
surfaced with plain snow, twisting between over-
grown banks.

On the near bank of the frozen creek the double
trail ended in a broad, trampled circle, centered
on a mound of something that was not entirely
snow.

Hurrying forward, looking over the deputy's
shoulder along the brilliant shaft of the
flashlight's beam, Joe could see blood. The trampled space was marked with it in little flecks and
splashes, fresh, not yet sanitized by falling snow.
And there, a pair of thick-lensed eyeglasses had
fallen. As they entered the circle Joe also saw a
human finger, its stump-end ragged and gory.
Had someone carried one of the poor kid's fingers
out here, meaning to hide evidence? Or—

The central mound was moving in the light. It
was sheepskin under newly fallen white. Joe
lifted at it with two hands, the deputy with the
hand in which he did not hold the light, and it
turned over.

"Jesus."

"He's still alive, anyway."

"Yeah."

Joe lifted some more, the deputy held his light
and brushed off snow. One arm in a sheepskin
sleeve fell dangling.

"Look at his hand."

"It's both hands. Jesus God."

Struggling to move the inert weight back toward the house, Joe found himself stepping on another loose finger. He saw a third. He didn't look for more. Halfway back to the house, the deputy started blasting on a whistle. In a few seconds his partner came running to them through the snow, gun drawn.

With three to carry they made quick work of getting the hurt man back into the house. Corday watched their entrance without comment, and slowly followed them to the bedroom. There they stretched their burden on the cot, the only feasible place.

Joe was angry. "You're a doctor, right? This is an emergency case we've got here, wouldn't you say?" But there was more to his anger than the fact that Corday was standing by so passively.

The two of them were at the bedroom doorway. One of the deputies squeezed past and ran out, evidently heading for the car radio again.

Corday said gently, imperturbably: "I will examine him if you wish." With Joe and the other deputy hovering watchfully, he approached the cot. He bent and touched the young man's face. The eyes of the supine figure opened, squinting, blinking like a newborn's in the light of the single lamp. It took those eyes a little while to focus on Corday's face.

Then the man on the cot raised what had been a hand. A gurgle came from his throat, and with a terrible effort he moved as if to rise, to scramble backward. Joe caught him under the armpits to keep him from falling to the floor, and in that moment the young man's body ceased to move.

Corday continued to regard the youth intently for a moment, without touching him again. Then he straightened. "Gentlemen, this man is dead."

"We're calling for an ambulance," the deputy argued, as if in contradiction. Meanwhile he was helping Joe lay the man down flat again. "Isn't there anything you can do? Heart massage . . . ?"

"It is too late."

The deputy stood indecisively for a moment. Then, mumbling swearwords, he stalked out after his partner.

The body on the cot certainly looked dead. Joe waited to hear the broken, grating sound with which the front door closed. Then he looked at the old man. "Dr. Corday?" His own voice was tighter than he liked. He felt close to some kind of violence himself. His anger was largely at himself, he realized, for being taken in.

"Yes, Joe?"

"I want you to tell me what happened to this man's hands. Don't tell me you should not like to venture an opinion."

The old man looked again at the figure on the cot. He was still cool, too cool. Only the crazies could be that cool. Joe should have seen it before.

Corday said: "It would appear that his fingers have somehow been—"

"Torn off, goddam it. I can see that. Who did it?"

"Discovering that would seem to be the job of the police. Though not necessarily, I suppose, of the Chicago Pawn Shop Detail?" Corday's voice was tired, as well as cool. That sounded like a request for a little more comradely co-operation.

No more. "This is the same guy who supposedly fired a gun at you?"

"Oh yes. Yes."

"He must have had his fingers then, right? Right? Then he ran out of here. Trying to get away? If he had the gun like you say, why was he running? And who chased him?"

A glint of something other than coolness came into the old man's eyes. Amusement, it looked like. "I would surmise that he ran to get to running water. A forlorn hope, of course. It would not have saved him. But still he was a more knowledgeable young man than some. About some things, at least."

"Running water, save him? What does that mean?" Joe knew he was losing his own coolness, his own control. The knowledge didn't help.

"Joe, believe it or not, I am extremely tired. I must rest before I undergo any lengthy questioning." Corday turned away to seek out the room's one chair. And pallor, tiredness, age, were indeed all showing in his face at the moment.

"Don't go to sleep just yet. I don't like that trick you pulled on me today, sending me off on a wild goose chase. I don't like a bunch of things about you. I'm not here as a cop tonight, and I can speak my mind." He immediately felt a little better, calmer, for having spoken that much of it at least. All right, he should have seen before that the old man had to be at least a little crazy.

Sitting wearily erect, hands on knees, Corday made the old chair almost a throne. "As for the wild goose chase, as you describe it, I would not have done that had there been time to win you over by argument. But there was no time. The boy had to be saved at once."

"You really knew that he was here. But how?"

"You saw."

Joe, the interrogating officer, stood over the seated suspect. "Let that pass for the moment. Let's go over again what you say happened here after you sent Judy and Johnny home. You were in the living room with this guy, he shot at you and then ran out. You stayed in the house. How do you suppose his fingers got torn off?"

Corday took a moment to ponder. "Perhaps, Joe, it would.be more profitable to start with *why*."

"All right, then. If you've got a good reason, try it out on me."

"There is revenge as a motive. You must come across that in your work."

"Not as often as you might think. Not like this. People do turn each other in to the police, there's plenty of that. If this was done for revenge, who did it?"

"Some—ally—of the Southerland family?"

"Who?"

"A second common purpose of torture," said the old man pedantically, "is of course the extortion of information. And a third purpose is to make an example of the victim. Perhaps to warn his associates to desist from a certain course of action—the persecution of a certain family, for instance."

Watching the old man, listening to him, Joe felt his earlier anger coming back, more coldly now. Eight years on the force, brushing now and then against every kind of evil that the city bred, had not prepared him for a close look at anyone like this. It was not what Corday might have done, or what he was saying, so much as what he was. Just what the old man was, Joe did not know; but the closer he got to it, the more his deepest feelings recoiled.

"Historically," the old man was continuing, "such frightful warnings have been more effective than many people currently suppose. Then of course, two or even all three purposes may be served by the same act—the same atrocity, if you will. And now, before you ask me another question Joe, will you answer one for me in turn?"

"I don't know. If I can. Maybe."

"Who is Craig Walworth?"

Joe blinked, trying to shift gears. "I've heard the name. Society. From one of the wealthy families in the city. What's he got to do with any of this? Don't tell me this is him?" He gestured at the still figure on the cot.

Corday shook his head tiredly. "I doubt that very much."

"This guy"—he gestured toward the cot, where blind blue eyes stared up—"ran down the hill to get to running water, huh?"

"Thinking his pursuer could not follow him across the stream. Grasping at a faint hope of that, at least."

"His pursuer, meaning you. The gun in your hand, not in his."

The wicked old eyes looking up at Joe were once more amused.

Joe shivered. Words came from him involuntarily: "I think you're crazy. You're a maniac. I should never have left Judy alone with you for a minute."

At last, at last, some basic feeling had been provoked, deep in those dark and ancient eyes that looked, to Joe, not a bit more human for its presence. Joe was suddenly, comfortingly, aware of the weight that rode his shoulder-holster, underneath his jacket. And it was a relief also to hear more cars arriving now, pulling in round the last turn of the long drive from the highway.

Thirteen

Again Judy was not alone in her own warm bedroom, though it was the middle of the night. Her waking was gradual and without fear, but she knew he was there even as she woke.

Judy turned over in bed and looked. This time his dark figure was standing beside the dressing-table chair.

"Have I alarmed you?" Dr. Corday's normal voice inquired softly.

"No." She sat up in bed, and was irritated to find herself involuntarily fingering the top button of her nightgown again. "What is it?"

"The truth is that I feel a need to talk. And I much prefer your company to that of anyone else I can talk with tonight."

"Won't you sit down?"

"Thank you." The chair in his hand moved with ghostly silence. He settled into it without a sound.

"I wanted to thank you," Judy said, "for what you did today."

"It was my pleasure, as well as my duty, to be of service." And her visitor made her a little seated bow.

"Can you tell me anything more about Kate?" When her question had gone unanswered for a moment Judy added: "I'm certain now that she's still alive. Don't ask me how I know. But I was right about Johnny, wasn't I? It's the same feeling."

"Indeed, you were right. You have a talent in such matters."

"But you don't want to talk about Kate yet. All right, I trust you."

He was silent for a time, and motionless in his chair. At last he said: "It is long, I think, since anyone has trusted me in such a way. Strange, it had not occurred to me for a long time, that I was never any longer trusted . . . ah, Judy, I am tired tonight."

"Can't you get any rest?"

"That is one thing I wished to discuss with you tonight. In the morning you will hear that I have disappeared from my motel. The police, as they believe, have put me in storage there, so they may check up on me with the authorities in London before they begin to question me intensively."

"Are you in trouble?"

He almost laughed, though not at her, she saw with relief. Perhaps at himself. "My dear! I am never out of trouble, one might say. Tomorrow the police will not find me available for questioning. But tomorrow night I shall be active again, and perhaps you will see me then. The task for which you so justly summoned me will be completed—if I can do it. The truth is, the enemy has proven to be rather more powerful than I at first suspected. Still, I believe I can succeed, if I am given occasional help as effective as your help was today."

"Oh yes! Anything. Of course. Do you have a place where you can rest?"

"Fortunately I long ago made preparations for a visit to the New World. You see, real rest is not always easy for me to obtain, particularly when I am this far from home. My enemies no doubt have counted on that fact. Oh, yes, it is my enemies that we are here concerned with."

"I don't understand."

"What is it about the Southerland family, I have asked myself, that could provoke such seemingly senseless attacks as those you have endured? The unique thing about the Southerlands, I say in answer to my own question, is their special relationship with a very unusual protector, an old friend no one else in America can claim. Ergo, the purpose of the seemingly purposeless onslaught is to lure this old friend of theirs here from across the sea. In America, his foes calculate, their chances of attacking him successfully will be much improved. Here, it will be hard for him to find a place to rest, and perhaps they can locate it when he does."

"And I called you here. I'm sorry. I never—"

"No! Do not be sorry for calling me. Even if I should be destroyed—which I do not for a moment mean to be."

"If you know who these enemies of yours are, we ought to let the police know too."

"It would not be easy to impress the truth upon

the police. Nor would it be wise. This is a private feud, best settled privately. We have made a start, one of our enemies is dead already."

"You mean the young man out at the house where Johnny was. I heard the police talking about all that. They were guessing about some strange kind of cult."

"I tried to explain something of the situation to Joe. He did not understand. But I believe you do. At least in part."

"That guy deserved to be killed!" Judy burst out. "When I think about my brother . . . you know we took Johnny to the hospital, under guard and all, and he still cried when I left him. Didn't want me to go. Was afraid they were going to get their hands on him again. Whatever happened to that fellow with the gun, he had it all coming to him."

Showing a little of his former energy, Corday got up to pace the floor. "We have at least three more foes who must be eliminated. And two of them are infinitely more dangerous than the one now dead, who was only their tool. I warn you, you who will at least begin to understand, that they have powers beyond anything you will expect a human being to possess."

"Not beyond yours."

He stopped in his pacing and they looked at each other silently. She could no longer see him as an old man. She felt torn between an impulse to jump out of bed and run to him, and a deeper urge, an inner warning even, to stay where she was.

He said: "In you I see . . . a fragment of my earlier self. And a young love."

"A young love? Is she still alive?"

"She? . . . ah yes, very much alive. In England." His teeth flashed in a smile, and the starlight or moonlight made it appear for a moment that something had gone wrong with their shape. "Will you know your own great love, when he appears?"

"At first sight, you mean? Oh, I'm not so foolish as to think that."

A little silence fell between them once again. The instinct that had warned Judy earlier now seemed to be signalling that the crisis, whatever it had been, was past. Under the covers she could feel her legs relaxing now, trembling slightly at the knees.

"I beg your pardon, Judy. I should not have spoken so patronizingly."

"I think you're a gentleman, Dr. Corday. You know, what people used to mean when they said someone was a gentleman. I don't know if I'm saying it right."

"I think I understand. I thank you."

"I'm glad I called you here. I don't understand how it worked, but I'm very glad I did."

"I also am glad." The tall figure in the gloom moved just a little closer. "Be brave, and we will win. I do not tell you not to be afraid."

"Are you ever afraid?" Then Judy shook her head. "I suppose that when fear ends, life is over."

In the dimness the expression on the tall man's face showed great tiredness, and now for a moment infinite sadness as well, so that for a moment Judy was frightened after all. And in the next moment, her visitor was gone.

Fourteen

The police artist was just packing up his sketch pads and getting ready to leave when Joe shepherded Judy and Clarissa past Johnny's police bodyguard in the hospital corridor and into the private room. The artist was chuckling a little as he packed, having evidently just made some little joke—or maybe Johnny was the joker, for here the kid was, sitting straight up in bed and looking well, or almost well, just as his mother and father had so thankfully described him.

A drift of vased and potted flowers and plants was mounting up at one side of the room, and two bedside tables were almost covered with cards and notes, along with some half-finished sketches that the artist had evidently abandoned. Johnny's hands were both heavily bandaged, and he held them out awkwardly behind first Judy's back and then Clarissa's when the women hurried to hug him.

When they took chairs at last, Joe moved up closer to the bed. "Well, buddy, you look a hell of a lot better than I expected."

"I feel real good, too." John appeared to pause to think about his feelings seriously. "Mom and Dad said I shouldn't have a bunch of visitors, but I hope you guys can stay a while."

"Cops have been bugging you with questions, I suppose."

"Oh, yeah, about the people who kidnapped me. They say the guy who stayed with me in the house is dead. They showed me a Polaroid of a dead man, and it was him, all right."

The kid seemed to be able to talk about it all quite lightly now. Wait, Joe thought, a reaction will hit him later. Nightmares at least. A little craziness of some kind, probably. The family will have to watch for it. He asked Johnny: "Who were the rest of them?"

"There were at least two other men, and one woman. And once, I swear, they had like a party going on. Whole bunch of people, talking in some weird foreign language."

"Huh."

"Yeah, I don't think the police and the FBI believe me either. They probably think I was delirious. But one night all these people were in the house, all talking what sounded like Latin."

"Latin," said Clarissa, as if shocked, as if the use of Latin in such a business would be some kind of special sacrilege. She sat back in her chair and looked at Judy, who only gave an impatient little headshake in reply.

John went on: "And the cops keep asking me if I ever got a message out, anything like that. I didn't.

I couldn't. How'd you ever know I was in there?"

Wishing that he hadn't quit smoking quite so permanently the last time, Joe bit at a hangnail. "I don't think I know the answer to that one myself."

Judy said defensively: "I keep telling everyone, I just had a feeling of where you were. First in a dream. And then, when Dr. Corday hypnotized me, I could find the house. I seemed to be able to really see you for a while, in that closet."

Mention of the closet made John give his head a twitchy shake. "Where's Dr. Corday now?" he wondered. "I asked Mom and Dad and they just sort of put me off. I'd like to be able to thank him."

Judy said: "He seems to have disappeared from his motel this morning." She sounded almost casual about it, which made Joe feel vaguely relieved.

Johnny's eyes widened. "I hope those guys didn't . . ."

"The kidnappers?" Joe shook his head. "I don't think so. The cops were watching the motel all night, I'm sure."

"Then how'd he get out?"

"That's a good question." Joe had his own ideas about that. His police instincts, if after eight years in the business you maybe began to have such things, told him that the old man had not looked at all like Dr. Corday when he came out, and furthermore Dr. Corday was not going to be easy to find again. Because Dr. Corday no longer existed. Disguises were generally nonsense, of course. But 'the kindly old family doctor from London' had itself been a disguise, one good enough to work, for a while anyway and among strangers. Except . . . Clarissa, of course. Granny Clare. Joe was going to have to talk to her in private when he got the chance. She hadn't met his eye directly all morning.

"Jeez, I hope he's all right." Johnny was starting to get upset about it.

"I'm sure he is," said Judy impulsively, sounding like there could be no doubt.

"I'm just as glad he's gone, myself," said Joe, and felt astonished at the violence of the glare that Judy turned on him.

She said: "He got my brother out of there."

"Yes, he did do that." Joe turned to the window, to study the grayness of middle-class Evanston in midwinter, through black skeletal trees. "Afterwards, though, Corday and I were talking, alone. The dead man was there on the cot in the same room. The deputies were out in their car using the radio. Corday was talking pretty crazy, then. I'm saying this because if he pops up again I think you all ought to use care in dealing with him."

"Crazy how?" Judy challenged.

"Well. Like it might very well have been him who killed that fellow, that way. Though he didn't confess it in so many words. To brag about something like that, whether you really did it or not . . . I've got to see Charley Snider later today and go over all of this with him."

Judy was angry. "If he killed a kidnapper, does that make him crazy?" Her brother was watching numbly. Clarissa was hiding her face, or maybe just resting her eyes.

Joe continued: "And then he said some incoherent-sounding things, like how the man

had run down the hill to get to running water.
That man's not normal . . . Clarissa, you all
right?"

"Running water," repeated Granny Clare,
through lips suddenly gone pale. Looking worse
than Johnny in his hospital bed, she started to get
up, clutched at a bedside table, sent papers spill-
ing to the floor. Then she sank back in her chair.

Judy, her normal self again, hurried to fuss over
her grandmother. Clarissa popped a nitoglycerin
pill, took some water, looked a lot better.

Joe asked: "Does running water mean anything
in particular?"

Judy scowled at him again, and turned to her
brother, changing the subject. "What did the
other people look like?"

"Oh. The only ones I really saw were the two
men in the car, the ones who grabbed me. I got the
best look at the one who was driving but he was
sort of ordinary-looking, I guess. See, I was walking along the side of Sheridan Road there, after
dark, coming home from the Birches', and this car
just pulled up slowly, and this guy with a dark
beard rolled down his window and asked for
some kind of phony directions. Then the back
door of the car opened, and this real monster sort
of jumped out. I didn't get much of a look at his
face, not then anyway, but man was he big. He was
the one who . . . "

John's voice trailed off. His eyes fell to his bandaged hands, and for a moment the boy's face
showed shock, as if it were just coming through to
him now what those bandages really meant. "I'll
be able to use my hands almost as good as ever,"

he added, with the air of doggedly repeating
something he had been told.

"You said there was a woman," Judy prodded,
probably just trying to snap Johnny out of his dark
contemplation.

He looked vacantly at his sister for a moment
before answering. "Yeah. There in the house, at
night. She looked into the closet at me, but it was
too dark for me to see her. I dunno. It's all kind of
vague." Suddenly turning into a hospital patient
after all, Johnny lay back on his pillows.

"I think we'd better let you rest." Judy bent over
her brother to hug him one more time.

When it came Joe's turn to say farewell, he
grinned at the boy and shook his own two hands
together. "Let us know if we can bring you anything."

"I will."

Judy had paused to restore the papers fallen
from the table. Looking at one sketch, she gave a
little sniff and almost smiled. "Know who this
looks like to me? I met him once, when he was
trying to get Kate to go on a skiing weekend with
him. Craig Walworth."

Fifteen

You didn't just find upper-crust society in the Chicago phone book, of course. But if you were in the police department you knew a number to dial to be told the address of someone with an unlisted phone.

Alone after dropping Judy and Clarissa off in Glenlake, driving on south toward the Loop's sky-notching towers, Joe considered for the dozenth time why he shouldn't just lay Craig Walworth's name on Charley Snider. The main reason, he decided, was his feeling that the evil old man wanted him to do just that. Why else had the old man brought the name up out of nowhere when they were alone? *Who is Craig Walworth?* Damn the old man to hell, anyway, for asking that and then disappearing. So there was no real Walworth-connection to be pointed out to Charley. One question, from someone who was very clever and not to be trusted; and one sketch that

140

might look a little like Craig Walworth but had evidently been discarded because it didn't look too much like the bearded kidnapper.

When they had given Joe his days off to mourn for Kate, they hadn't specifically warned him to keep from muddling up the Southerland investigations by doing any poking around on his own. The captain evidently hadn't thought him dumb enough to need a warning of that kind. Well, he wasn't dumb. And he wasn't getting into the investigation, he told himself now. He was only trying to get it clear in his own mind whether there might be anything that could tie Craig Walworth into it.

While driving Judy home he had questioned her casually—as casually as he could manage—about that skiing weekend invitation. Judy had been very definite that Kate had never accepted any proposition like that from Craig Walworth. But Judy would say that now, anyway, just to spare Joe's feelings.

When he reached the tall apartment building on Lake Shore Drive, Joe had a qualm about using his police ID to get in. He compromised by using it and then telling the doorman he wanted to see Walworth on personal business. The doorman, an old-timer whose badly fitting jacket suggested he might just have been called out of retirement, told him, sure lieutenant, that's okay, I'll watch your car, just leave it in the drive. I'll just give him a buzz to let him know you're coming. Oh, yes, the ID helped.

Joe went up alone in the small elevator, up to a small marbled foyer where someone's old rain-coat hung covering a mirror or picture. He touched a bell button beside a dark door of massive wood, that reminded him of yesterday's broken-in front door. A lean old fellow like Corday, wiry-strong or not, could hardly have done that without a sledge . . . .

Walworth himself came to answer the door. And Judy had been right about the sketch, it hadn't been far off at all in depicting this man's face. The dark hair and even the short beard were messed up now. Walworth was wearing a loose, short, very fancy robe of some kind, his hairy, muscular arms and legs protruding. He had the look of someone just out of bed, even to the puffiness around the eyes. He also looked a little jumpy. But a great many perfectly innocent people looked jumpy when you came on as the police.

"If you're a cop," said Walworth in a voice whose loudness sounded habitual, "come in and get it the hell over with, whatever it is."

"Thanks." Joe came in, let Walworth close the door behind him. The palatial apartment was a littered mess, evidently from last night's party. "But like I said, it's not police business. I just wondered if I could have a word with you about Kate. Sorry I got you up."

"Kate?" The dumb look might be genuine.

"Kate Southerland."

"Oh. Oh, yeah. Sure. Terrible. What can I tell you? I hardly knew her." Walworth picked up a half-empty bottle, frowned at it, put it down. No doubt the maid, or a battalion of maids, would soon be along to see that it was disposed of.

Joe said: "You see, I had asked her to marry me."

"Oh," said Walworth, and his face went

through several changes of expression, the first of which looked like genuine surprise. None of the expressions seemed likely to be helpful. "I'm very sorry," he thought of saying finally.

"Yeah. Well, I just wondered if you could tell me about what happened that last night she was here." Joe had designed this question, or statement, with great care, and had rehearsed it on the long drive down from Glenlake.

"Here?" For a moment, consternation. "But she was never *here*."

Joe had also rehearsed his next step, to be taken after this anticipated denial; but before he could put his plans for further probing into effect, he heard a door opening and closing somewhere down a hallway.

"Craig?" The one tentative word in a softly feminine voice preceded the girl around a corner and into the room. She came wearing a cloud of red hair almost the color of fresh copper wire, and a large green towel wrapped around her body from armpits to hips. She had a green-eyed pixie face, with an upturned, freckle-sprinkled nose that made her look so young that *statutory jailbait* was the first thought—or anyway the second— that sprang into Joe's police-trained mind. But she could have been six months or a year past eighteen.

"Craig?" Her voice was still soft but Joe could tell now, watching her sober face, that there was intense anger driving it. "Where did you put my clothes?"

Walworth gave Joe a look that seemed to be meant as an appeal for man-to-man solidarity in this situation. Then, shaking his head, the host walked out of the room in the direction the girl had come from.

Now looking at Joe, the girl in the green towel announced, in a different though still distant voice: "My name is Carol."

"I'm Joe."

"Joe, could I ask you to give me a lift? It won't be very far."

"Sure. I've got a car."

Carol continued to look at him, as if daring him to try to say something about the towel. He had nothing funny available, even if he had wanted to try. He walked over to one floor-to-ceiling window and looked out through the thick protective glass at the Drive twenty stories below, a strip of snowbound park beyond, and then the winter-blackened lake, a rim of white of snow and broken ice extending outward from the shore a hundred yards or so. A very dull December day. What was it, Wednesday?

He would try to pump the girl a bit before he decided whether to come back to Walworth, or to give Walworth's name to Charley Snider, or just what to do.

In about one minute Walworth was back in the room, carrying an armful of assorted garments. Wordlessly Carol accepted these, meanwhile maintaining her towel's position carefully. Then she went out the way that she had come, silent pink feet sinking into carpet. Her legs were very nice.

Walworth paced the floor, showing no inclination to say anything more to Joe. Once he stopped to pick up a stray bottle, take a drink from it and grimace. All right, Joe told him silently, you've answered my question. You'll find out about it if I decide your answer doesn't stick.

Before Joe had begun to expect her, Carol was back in the living room with them, wearing boots and jeans and a carefully faded, expensive-looking shirt: what the wealthy wear when they want to look like they don't care. She went straight to the guest closet, took out a hip-length ski jacket, went through its pockets, came up empty.

"My money?" she demanded then, of Walworth's back.

He turned right around, not having to pause for an instant. "What d'you charge?"

That stung enough to show for just a moment in her face. "I mean the money that was in my pockets when I came in here last night."

"I don't know." He glared at her brutally. "Look around for it, if you want. Or if you don't want to miss your ride, come back later and maybe it'll have turned up."

"For eight dollars I'm not going to stay here long enough to look around." She pulled her jacket on, turned to Joe. "Not for eight hundred. Can I have that ride now?"

Wishing he could think of comebacks that quickly, Joe just managed to have the door open as she reached it. A last glance back as they went out showed Walworth picking up a bottle again.

"Don't like him, do you?" Joe remarked, when they had ridden the elevator halfway down.

"Not at a second look." Carol's manner had relaxed a little as soon as they got out of the apartment. "Met him last Friday for the first time. Oh, he can come on very strong and decent when he tries. Then last night—that was something else. I'd rather not talk about it."

"Sure." The elevator delivered them. The gray-haired doorman smiled and nodded. Joe led her out to the Rabbit in the drive.

She said: "I don't know what your business with him was, but I got definite vibrations that you don't like him either. Which is why I took a chance on asking for a ride."

"You're right, I don't like him. So, where shall the ride be to?"

"The Art Institute, if it's not out of your way. I hear a girl can pick up a better class of man there than in the bars."

"I suppose they might be better educated, anyway." He pulled out of the drive and melded into traffic gently, heading south.

After two blocks Carol said: "No, I don't want to pick up men. One stab at that was plenty. I'm going to have to think of something, though, being entirely out of money."

"I'm not trying to be funny when I say, how about Travelers Aid? Really. You do have the look of someone who's some distance from home, and they'll help you wire someplace for money. Or I'll advance you a loan myself. But it'll have to be small."

"I'm afraid—" Carol's voice cracked suddenly in the middle, and she had to start it over. "I'm afraid sending out wires isn't going to do me any good. Thanks for the offer of the small loan. I may just accept. Could we start out with a coffee someplace?"

"Joe's Coffee Shop and Breakfast Bar is open.

That's my place, which is not terribly far. Or we can go public if you like."

"Joe's place sounds fine. It's got to be a lot nicer than the one I just got out of."

He turned west for two blocks, then back north. "I'm a little out of the high rent district, as they say."

There was a legitimate parking spot open only half a block from his front door, so he didn't have to drive through the alley to his rented garage. While they were climbing the stairs to the second floor of his building, he could hear the muffled sound of his phone ringing, and ran ahead to answer.

"Joe? This's Charley Snider."

"What's up, Charley?"

"Just wanted to bring you up to date. Nothing new on the mystery at the morgue. But, we finally did get a make on the thumbprint on the mirror in Kate's car. Now don't get your hopes up. You said you wanted to know anything that happens, and so I'm calling to tell you."

Joe didn't feel in any danger of getting too much hope up about anything. "What about the print?"

"Well, the name the FBI files come up with is Leroy Poach. Pee-oh-ay-cee-aitch, as in egg. And now, get this man, I'm not makin' this up. Murder, armed robbery, kidnapping." Charley paused, as before a climax.

"Yeah?"

"The thing is, this Poach was hanged in Oklahoma in 1934."

"Oh, Jesus. Are they crazy in Washington?" By now Carol had come into the apartment, and was standing by in the next room, politely not listening. Joe caught her eye and made gestures toward the kitchen alcove. She brightened a little, and moved in that direction.

"Well," said Charley's phone-voice, "there's obviously some mistake. If it turned out somehow that he wasn't hanged, he'd still be about eighty-five by now."

"Well. I did ask you to tell me everything."

"Hey, now, don't quit on us. We're tryin'."

"I know. I'm sorry." Sounds from outside the bedroom indicated Carol was filling the coffeepot. "Charley? What does running water mean?"

"Huh?"

"Why was that fellow out at the house running down there into the woods along the creek?"

"I dunno. Oh, by the way, we got his name now. Max Gruner. Has a minor record, sex offenses, larceny. We don't know what he's been up to the last six months or so, but it looks like it wasn't anything good. And the house, you know, where the kid was being held? It belongs to some people who moved away last fall. They're down south now, and they've been paying a couple to come round and look at the place every day. Only the caretakers have just up and disappeared. Sweet setup for a kidnapping hideout."

Joe asked: "Anything on Corday yet?"

"Seems to have left his things in the motel room and just departed. His bill was paid in advance. We've checked with London, and they don't know him. Hasn't been practicing medicine in London, not under that name anyway, not legitimately. Might have been living there, of course.

His name was listed on a BOAC flight into O'Hare from London a few days back."

"I bet you don't find him, Charley."

"Any ideas where he might be, Joe?"

"I don't have any sane ideas about any of this right now. If any come to me I'll pass them along."

They said goodbye and he hung up and went out into the dining alcove. Carol had set out a couple of paper plates and was scrambling some eggs.

She looked at him. "I couldn't help hearing. The name Corday and all, that's been in the news. I think I just had a lot of the air let out of my own troubles, because it just hit me, who this girl is, that you told Walworth you were going to marry. God. Craig knew her too?"

He went to pour boiling water into the two cups where she had spooned in instant coffee. "Slightly, anyway. Tell me about last Friday night up there at Walworth's."

"Oh. That's when I met him. I was there most of the evening, but I don't recall any girl who fits my picture of Kate Southerland. Describe her to me?"

When he had done so, Carol shook her head. "No. Unless she could have been there earlier, six o'clock or so."

"She was still home then."

The eggs and some toast were ready, and they were just sitting down when the phone sounded again. He went to the bedroom, sat down heavily on the bed, picked it up. "Joe Keogh."

"Joe?" It was Granny Clare's voice, sounding tremulous. "Are you—is everything all right?"

"Yeah. Why not? No new disasters, anyway. Why? Is everything all right there?"

There was a small delay before Clarissa answered, but when she did she sounded definite. "Yes. I . . . oh, I shouldn't have bothered you. I'm sorry. Good-bye." And she hung up.

Some of the modest portion of food on Carol's plate was gone when he came back. She had already set down her fork. "I think what I mainly am is tired. I've just been through a night you wouldn't believe."

"I might." Joe sat down opposite, took a bite of toast, discovered he was mildly hungry. "I've recently been through an unreal thing or two myself."

She sat with arms folded, looking over his shoulder. "I'm sorry if you don't want to hear this, but I don't think I can keep from talking about it after all."

"Go ahead." He tried to sound no more than willing.

"I was up there at Walworth's for a long time Friday night. There was some sex going on, okay? Too kinky to interest me. Somehow Craig gave me the impression then that it wasn't really his thing either. Then, last night, I went up with him, thinking we were going to be alone. All right, I was planning to spend the night. But what he had in mind was . . . well, nothing I'd consider ordinary, and I don't think my life has been especially sheltered."

"How old are you, Carol?" he asked her, almost without meaning to.

"Old enough, in the legal sense." But he had brought her story-telling to a halt.

"All right, go on, sorry I interrupted."

"Well. He turned out to be kinkier than I had thought, that's all. And it wasn't until after my clothes were off and had been misplaced somewhere that this was fully explained to me. Hell, why am I telling you all this?"

"Because it bothers you."

"That's for sure. Then there were arguments. There were some other people around, by that time . . . not Kate, no one as nice as Kate, I'm sure. Oh, I'm dead. I don't know if I'm going to fall asleep first or start to cry."

"You can do either one. Or both. But eventually I think you ought to tell me where you live, really live, so I can see that you get home."

"I don't think so. Oh, damn. Every time I shut my eyes some tears come squeezing out."

"I do think so. Really. Is home that bad?"

"No," she said, surprising him a bit. "My parents live right in Chicago, actually. All right, let me give them a call."

"Help yourself to the phone."

She went into the bedroom, and he could hear her dialing. Now soon she would be gone. He didn't quite know exactly what he thought of that. He drank some coffee. He thought he heard her once say *Daddy* on the phone—he couldn't make out what else she might be saying, but at least it didn't sound like a fight.

In a couple of minutes she hung up and came out again, looking more relaxed than he had seen her yet. "Joe, can you give me one more ride? It's only about ten minutes away."

"Okay. Were your parents glad to hear from you?"

"Oh, you know how it is. But that's a silly thing to say, isn't it? Maybe you don't know how it is at all."

He smiled at her. "No, I guess I don't."

Back in the car, she directed him toward the Near North Side. It was actually the same general area as the half-abandoned building where Kate had been found dead, an area in which a few blocks one way or the other made a big difference in what the city was like.

ENCHANTRESS COSMETICS, said the sign, discreet but expensive bronze. It was on a modern gray concrete building, two stories high, that occupied almost half a square block.

"You live here?"

"It's the family business, or the office and laboratory ends of it anyway, with living quarters attached. My folks think it's a lot neater than commuting, or living in one of those high-rise apartments."

He had heard of a few other wealthy people in the area, advertising agency owners and such, who had made similar arrangements. "It sounds neat."

A private automobile entrance was blocked by a great openwork gate of what looked like blackened steel and ebony. This rose up out of the way when Carol worked some kind of miniaturized electronic device she brought out of a pocket. Good thing, Joe remarked to himself, she hadn't lost that in her recent adventurings.

Inside, below street level, were private parking spaces, one or two out of a dozen of them occupied. From the sunken garage a large but fancy elevator very silently raised them to the floor above.

At the far end of a small, carpeted hall, another doorway was fitted with a wood-and-metal gate. This one stood open, and beyond it a luxurious though badly lighted apartment was visible. Silhouetted in the doorway was a man, very large, well-dressed, smiling at them both.

"Goodbye," Joe said to Carol, taking her hand just briefly.

"Don't say goodbye." Her smile was warm.

"So long for a while, then. How about that?"

"Not even that," she said. "You must come in for a visit." She turned to flash the well-dressed man a merry wink.

Joe looked from one of them to the other. He wanted to smile at them but couldn't quite. "Your father?" he asked, then realized that the man who was strolling toward them looked too young for that.

"Oh, goodness, not at all." Carol's green eyes danced, as if with some joke soon to be revealed. "Does the name Enoch Winter mean anything to you, Joe?"

"Enoch Winter. No." the huge man was looming beside him now. A joke was coming. Or something was—

"Then how about—Leroy Poach?" And she giggled brightly, watching the slow progress of his reaction.

On the threshold of the luxurious apartment Carol and the giant man had laughed at him. Still laughing, the giant had reached for Joe in a lei-

surely, careless way. There had been nothing at
all funny in the power of the grip that closed on
Joe's right arm. He had let go at once with a left
hook that landed square on the other's jaw. The
only effect was a shock of pain through Joe's fist,
as if he had hit a wall. With that Carol stepped in
and caught Joe by the left arm. She was still
amused. Between them the two of them carried
his kicking figure into the apartment as if he were
an obstreperous two-year-old.

Inside, a vista of elegant though poorly lighted
rooms seemed to stretch away for half a block.
Carol closed a solid wood-and-metal door behind
them, while the man held Joe by both arms. The
man stood in front of him, grinning, daring him
silently. When the girl left them, walking unhur-
riedly into another room, Joe tried again. Wrenching free was hopeless, clumsy though the other's
grip appeared to be. When Joe tried for a kick, the
man with overwhelming power simply forced
him lower. Joe's knees buckled.

"Yeah, I know you're a cop, sonny," the man
said, in answer to a choked-out, embarrassingly
feeble protest. "I like the idea of you being one. I
really do."

He then let go of Joe's arms so suddenly that his
victim was left off balance and did a prat-fall on
the thick carpet. "All right, pull out the gun." The
huge man's voice was perilously soft. "Go on."

In eight years he'd never drawn it, except on the
firing range. He was ready to use it now, except
the big guy was just too willing. Some fighter's
instinct warned Joe to choose another tactic.
There was a small end-table within arm's reach,
and as Joe crouched to get up he seized it by one

leg. Whipping it ahead of him as he rose, he jabbed it into the giant's face as hard as he could. He got the surprise he wanted, and felt the table connect with what ought to have been a knockout impact.

But his opponent came at him right through the blow. Again Joe scrambled backward; the table was knocked from his grasp. Now he tried in earnest to draw his gun, but the quickness of his enemy was as incredible as his strength, and again Joe's arm was caught before his fingers could reach the holster.

This time, it seemed, the arm might in fact be twisted off—

"Stop!" The sharp command in the woman's voice brought the torture to a halt. Joe was dropped to the floor, where he rolled helplessly for a moment, trying to verify that nothing in his arm was broken or seriously torn.

Somewhere above him, Carol lectured. "The object is to learn something from him, remember?"

"Whatta you want to learn? He'll tell us."

"I want him to speak to us freely, Poach. Giving little details that will be clues, though he may not realize it. And I want to waste none of his sweet blood, if we can help it." Her voice, that had begun normally, ended in a ghastly whisper, and long before she had finished speaking, Poach had moved away. Joe, getting shakily to his feet, could see the other man's forehead marked with an almost straight horizontal line, oozing red. Poach dabbed at his hurt with a finger, looked back at Joe with the eyes of a wounded predator.

But Carol was standing between them now, a

hypodermic in her hand. "I have a little something here for you, Joe. It will only make you sleepy. Are you going to be a sensible young man and let me do it? Or are you going to try again to—"

He tried again. Ten seconds later he had a few more minor bruises, had discovered that a heavy metal ashtray made no more impression on either of his foes than kuckles did, and was being held down like an infant atop a great wooden table, a drafting or designing table of some kind, one place in the room where lights were bright. He could feel his shirt and jacket being peeled back partially from one shoulder. About all he could see from under an elbow that held his head immobilized, face down, was part of the nearest wall. What appeared to be a pair of harpoons were mounted there, crossed diagonally like fencing foils. Crude, early harpoons perhaps; even their heads were wood, or looked like wood, with pointy wooden barbs. . . .

The needle stung him in the shoulder and almost at once the world dissolved into a fog, a haze through which two pale faces hovered over Joe. One was haloed by red hair, the other blued with gun-metal stubble and blooded with a forehead crease. Both of them were made gigantic by his own helpless terror.

"Where is the old man, Joe? You know who I mean."

He knew who she meant, all right, but nothing more. If he had, he would have told her. He had been relieved of all choice in what he said.

Carol was gentle and understanding. "If you

don't know where he is now, Joe, tell us where you saw him last."

"That house . . . out in the country . . . the night we. . . ."

"The night Gruner was killed. Yes. And where before that?"

His mouth worked by itself. All he had to do was lie there on the table and observe the process. He mentioned the Southerland house, the parking lot of the Shores Motel, the Loop, the mausoleum in Lockwood Cemetery. . . .

"Enough," said Carol when he started to repeat himself, and his mouth shut up at once. She turned to Poach. "That mausoleum ought to be worth a try. First, do you know where Lockwood Cemetery is? And, second, can you check it out before sunset? Do not try to meet him alone at night."

"You tell me that about twice a day."

"Because I don't think you believe me, Poach. Look up the cemetery on the city map."

"Okay, okay. Then what about the house? We got to try to get in there sometime."

"Yes, the house too, today. If—"

"Before sunset. I know. I'm on my way."

Sixteen

Sitting up in bed, Craig Walworth could feel on one side of his throat the paired coolnesses of two fresh drops of painless blood. No mirror at hand to see them in, but he knew from past experience they were so small that touching them would mark his finger with red specks barely visible.

"A couple of months ago," he remarked, "you couldn't have convinced me it was possible for people to really get their kicks doing this. I mean relatively normal people."

Carol had just rolled away from him and now her naked body lay curved in a far quadrant of the huge circular bed, her flame of hair almost covering an outsize pillow. Beyond her the unshaded window, twenty stories above observation, looked out upon great clouds above the lake, clouds painted now with the reflection of a sunset developing in the opposite direction.

Carol gave one of her little laughs. She had

them in several styles, and this particular style, Walworth was slowly coming to realize, was derisive. She said: "You consider yourself relatively normal, darling?"

"I guess I do, though I'm not proud of it."

"Anyway, two months ago is just about when we first met. And it didn't take me long at all to convince you that vampirism really works."

"I mean, no one could have convinced me by argument. Demonstration was what did the trick." The sensations accompanying her sipping from his veins were more diffuse than those of any other sex act he had ever performed, but nonetheless orgasmic. "And one of the points I like best is that we can alternate this vampire act with going at it in the more traditional ways. You never seem to take enough blood to leave me weak, or anything. One of these days, my love, we're going to try both at once, and what a hit that'll be."

"I think it's time we got up," said Carol, ignoring everything he had said.

"I still don't get just how you do it. I mean, make tiny punctures like this with just your teeth. I can see you'd have to have teeth like needles. It never hurts a bit and the holes are so small. But your teeth don't look the least bit odd. I've had my tongue in there between 'em too, not to mention—"

"Don't be gross." Her voice cutting him off was cold, but then she winked. "I really do think it's time we jumped up and got dressed."

"What's the hurry?"

"There are things to do tonight. Things are going to be happening."

"What things? Goddam it, you can answer me. How do you do the biting?"

"Just like in the movies," she said, and rolled out of bed on her side and started to pull on her dress. Nothing under it, of course; cold never seemed to bother Carol.

"Movies?"

"Vampire movies. Craig dear, don't be dense. Now *will* you dress?"

"If it's that easy I ought to be able to do it to you too."

From the top of the green dress emerged green eyes, looking at him coldly. "I do not enjoy having my throat bitten," Carol stated. "Anyway, tasting my blood would change you too fast. You are perfect just the way you are. I wish to enjoy you and use you just a little longer yet."

He stretched out with hands behind his head, thinking to himself how nicely his big biceps showed in this position. "You're using me, huh? When are you going to get over your hangups about my mirrors?" The large glass on the nearest wall had been sprayed opaque, like a store window at Halloween; there were only a few scars in the ceiling to show where his overhead mirror had been taken down completely, at Carol's insistence, before she would mount the round bed with him.

"Sometime soon, I think," she answered, seriously enough to surprise him a little. She was sitting in a chair now, gracefully putting on a shoe. "I think you're ready."

"You do a good act about the mirrors," he said. "Never explicitly explaining why. Just putting these out of action, and covering up the one in the lobby with that raincoat. Leaving it to me to make the connection with the fairy-tale vampires who won't show up in a mirror."

Shoes on, Carol had stood and turned away to watch the sunset-reflecting clouds. "Big storm's coming," she remarked, as if to herself. Then she turned back. "Tell me more about the fairy-tale vampires."

"Well, you know. You do it well."

"I think I'd better be blunt," Carol said. "When have you ever actually seen my reflection in a mirror? I really do want to have you around a while longer, and you're not going to last unless you start to understand some things. In fact, you may not last out the night."

"What's all this," Walworth demanded, starting to get angry, "about how I'm going to be used?" She had never talked like this to him before; he realized now that some kind of a crisis in their relationship was at hand. "If you've got any ideas about turning me over to that dumb Irishman as a kidnapper, forget them. You and King Kong are in this just as deep as I am, remember. If that kid ever identifies me as driving the car, your ass has had it too."

"Craig, don't ever let Winter hear you call him that." Carol issued the warning calmly but seriously, a stewardess telling you to put on the belt. "As for that dumb Irishman, as you call him, he won't be coming around again. That was well played, darling. You do have talents outside of bed."

Walworth was still lying in the same position. "So, what'd you do? Pay him off? Kill him? I'd like to know about it. I mean, I'd really like to know, dearie, if you're killing people and it might someday involve me. An hour later you were back here. Did you take him home and bite his neck?"

Carol seemed to be considering her answer seriously. Meanwhile she was straightening her dress around her, fluffing out her hair. She did, now that he thought about it, have the habit of doing such things without mirrors. At last she said: "No, I haven't bitten his neck. Not yet. Anyway, it's not really the police you have to worry about."

"It's not? That's a pretty good one."

"No it isn't, dear. It wasn't the police who pulled off Gruner's fingers."

"Obviously. I know who that was. Your psychopathic playmate Winter or whatever the hell you think I ought to call him. Who else does things like that? But if he ever comes after me, baby, he's not going to get within arm's length of me alive."

"It was not M'sieu Winter who did it, either. Please get up and dress.

"Why should I?" But there was a certain psychological disadvantage in nakedness when she stood there like a nurse, so before it could become a real issue Walworth got out of bed and started rooting for some clothes. He said: "You're too smart to stick with a crazy like him. So why try to cover up for him with me, of all people?"

"I am not covering up. It is just that I still need Winter for a while, or at least I would like to be able to use him."

"Just like me," he mocked.

"Exactly. So please, Craig, can you take seriously the warning I am about to give you?

Whether or not you are arrested is almost of no consequence any more—"

"Don't pretend you're crazy, baby! I know better." He jiggled himself into his pants, pulled up the zipper.

"—but there is a certain old man you must look out for, Craig. Of course he may not look like an old man when you see him . . . " Carol sighed prettily, a concerned nurse whose patient just will not co-operate. "I'm really not getting through, am I? I was considering sending Winter over to be your bodyguard for a while, but now I don't think I'd better."

Walworth snorted, tucking his shirt into his pants. He decided to leave the shirt open halfway down the front. "Damn right you hadn't better. What is all this shit, all of a sudden? 'Don't bother to worry about the cops, Craig.' 'You may not last out the night anyway, Craig.' *I'll* last out the night, baby. 'Be nice to Winter, Craig.' You're setting up something. Hey, is this where you try at last to stick it to me for some money? Enchantress Cosmetics not making a profit after all?"

There was an edge in Carol's voice now. "Don't give me any money, please. I probably have more than you."

"Hah."

"But do watch out for the old man. He is the one who pulled off Gruner's fingers. He may well be coming after you tonight. I'm sure Gruner must have told him your name."

"And yours too, huh?" Walworth smiled, unable to concentrate enough to decide which shoes he ought to wear; this was really getting entertaining.

"He knows my name already. He's mentioned in the news stories, by the way, as a Dr. Corday of London. He's called himself that before."

"Oh? So, who is he really, Al Capone?"

"I see now you would only laugh like an idiot if I tried to tell you his real name, so never mind. Among other things he is an old friend of the Southerland family. And a very old enemy of mine."

Sitting on the bed with one sock half on, Walworth paused. "You're telling me, in this newly devious way of yours, that it's not an accident after all that we picked the Southerlands."

"Not a bit of an accident." Carol folded her arms. She was not a nurse any more; maybe the president of a company.

"Now wait a minute. The object was, we were going to look for some new kicks, right? Pick out a family and just utterly destroy them. An ultimate kick, better than just a simple killing. Right?"

"So it was presented to you at the time. So you thought you were presenting the idea to me."

"All right, say the idea was something you conned me into. Picking the Southerlands as the target must have been at random. Winter tore a page out of the Glenlake phone book—"

"A selected page."

"All right, say you fixed that too. Then I pinned the page up on the wall myself, and you stood clear across the room and tossed the dart. Don't tell me you could have hit a name on purpose from that distance. Hell, you couldn't even have seen it. You were lucky to hit the page, even."

"I can do many things, Craig, that you would not credit as being possible. So can the old man. I think I may send Winter over, after all, when he gets back."

"I may not let him in."

Carol stared at him a long moment, different emotions contending in her face. Then it was as if she gave up. Fought to keep herself from dissolving in laughter, but had to yield at last. "Oh, Craig, Craig, but you are such an innocent! Haven't you yet understood the first simple truth about me? And the man you know as Winter? We are *vampires*, dear. You've asked us both in here already. Do you think that you can now simply tell us to stay out, and we will?"

Walworth stood up in his socks. He had a growing feeling of unreality, and if he thought about it, he would have to admit that fright was growing too. "I've got a gun. I tell you, I'll blow that bastard Winter's head off, right on my own doorstep if I have to." The police would then come down on him for sure. His connection with the kidnapping would almost certainly come out, and he would be fighting in a courtroom for his life. Somehow he had always felt sure that, sooner or later, things would come to that.

She was calm and almost pleasant again. "Go get your gun, Craig dear. Right now. I want to show you something."

He looked his uncertainty at her.

"Oh, all right, never mind the pistol. It would probably only complicate things anyway. You'd think we had loaded it with blanks, or something. Just watch this."

And saying that, Carol disappeared, green dress and red hair and pink skin just swirling away to nothing. Not from a position where there was anything at all to hide behind: from right in the middle of his bedroom floor.

PCP, Walworth thought at once. He'd seen the elephant tranquilizer hit like this before, with heavy hallucinations. Not on himself, of course. He'd never used it on himself. But now Carol or someone had sneaked it into his food or drink. Intending to get rid of him . . . no, not in his food, an injection, that was it. A mainliner right into the jugular, managed somehow by Carol when she was supposed to be drinking his blood. No wonder she hadn't wanted mirrors around the bed . . .

A spring-loaded panel in the wall near the head of his bed, a movieish gadget that no one would expect to come across in real life, delivered his .38 into his hand as he reached out and pressed the wood. He was reasonably sure that neither Carol nor Winter nor the maids nor anyone else who had been in the apartment recently knew that it was there; it had been installed a year ago, and he hadn't spoken of it to any of them—not even of the gun until just now. Nevertheless he suspiciously broke the revolver's action open, slid the faintly oily cartridges one by one out of the cylinder and weighed them in his fingers, looked at them and tamped them gently back. Firing pin was in place too. He snapped the weapon shut, ready for business. The thing looked and felt awfully functional.

From behind him, from the direction of the huge bedroom window, there sounded a brisk, light tapping, as of something very hard striking on glass. Even as Walworth turned it seemed to him that he knew already, in some nightmare-hatching inner corner of his mind, just what it was that he was going to see.

Carol's face hovered close outside the almost unbreakable glass, twenty stories in the air. Her feet were extended toward the lake. With lightly moving arms she swam, a great smiling fish in an immense aquarium . . . then she was gone again.

"How was that?" her voice asked, once more from behind him, this time from in the room. Before turning again, he noticed that the night-backed glass showed him a half-reflection of the lighted bedroom—but not of Carol.

He spun around again then, to face her across the wide, round bed. "Bitch." His voice was low and murderous. "You stuck me with a good one, didn't you?"

"Stuck you?" She pretended not to understand. "I see you found your pistol. If you think it will protect you against Winter, or the old man, then fire it at me. Right now."

She sounded too eager. Whatever her game was, he wasn't going to play it. He shook his head. But in his anger he moved toward her. He was expecting that when he got close enough she would try to kick him where it would hurt the most. He was expecting that and ready for it. But only when he swung his arm to club her with the pistol barrel did she move, and then only to lift her arm. Her little palm caught his forearm, and it felt like he had swung at a cast-iron statue.

And almost before the pain of the impact had had time to register, Carol had grabbed him by both elbows, picked him up, and spun him in mid-air like some casually victimized infant. She spun him once more, in reverse, and ended the mad ballet by throwing him contemptuously into a chair, which nearly tipped over as he landed. He sat there blinking at her stupidly, for the moment unable to do anything more.

"You utter goddamned fool," she said, and added something in the same withering tone, but in a language he did not know. She finished up in English: "I wash my hands of you."

His rage had reached the point where his body acted of itself. His arm came up and fired the gun point-blank. The sound reverberated, the smell of burnt explosive stung his nose, the fruitwood table behind Carol leaped up against the wall and came down on its side. She stood there, icily contemptuous.

At his elbow the phone was ringing.

He debated whether to fire at her again. She waited, perhaps also debating something in her own mind.

Five rings, six.

He reached out his left hand and picked it up.

Winter's voice, rough, excited, incoherent.

Carol came near him and snatched the phone away. Walworth spun away out of his chair, not wanting her to touch him now, and afraid of what she might do if she did touch him.

"Are you sure?" she said into the phone, What she heard from it then transformed her into a goddess of victory, standing tall with head flung back. "Are—you—sure—that—it—was—him?" Her lips looked rigid, driving the words like nails into the phone.

The answer this time brought from Carol an outcry that sounded as if she had been hurt. But Walworth could see in her face that it was triumph. He backed away a little farther, sat down on the bed.

"No!" she was saying into the phone now. He had never seen anyone so beautiful. "In that case he should be kept alive—yes, yes, yes, *alive*, until later, when I can get to him. Later tonight. No, the gathering is at my place, within the hour. Leave him where he is, and come to my place. Yes, right away."

Very carefully she replaced the receiver in its cradle on the little table, near the bed. Walworth sat very still. A Carol he had never seen before looked down at him.

"Maybe, darling, just maybe—you will survive the evening after all. And I suppose you had better, after all, watch out for the police. Until later, dear."

With that, Carol was gone again.

As she disappeared, Walworth had been staring with fascination at a spot near the center front of the green dress. A small hole the size a bullet might make was there, showing a glimpse of pink, undamaged skin.

After a while, when he could begin to believe that he was really alone, he got up and looked at the fruitwood table where it lay on one side against the wall. A great splintered gouge had entered its top from underneath and emerged through the upper surface of the wooden top, where something had passed with tremendous force. Plaster had trickled from a small crater in the wall just behind where the table had been standing.

Walworth, gun still in hand, walked to the front door of the apartment, where he made sure that the door was securely locked, chained, and bolted. The only other way in, unless you counted the sealed windows, was the service door in the kitchen. That was his next stop.

Then he went into a bathroom, and in the mirror over the sink examined the small wounds on his throat. They looked no different from the marks Carol had left him with the other times. They could be needle punctures. They were needle punctures, and he was a fool not to have realized that fact the first time round, or anyway the second.

Syringes capable of injecting drugs hidden in her teeth? It sounded like something from a crazy spy adventure. He had set down the revolver on the broad ledge beside the bathroom basin, and now he suddenly grabbed it up and spun around again, in expectation of hearing her contemptuous voice once more.

But there was nothing. Now he hurried through the apartment shutting the drapes on all the windows. At times he ran from room to room, wanting to get them shut before he could be made to see her swimming out there once again.

When he had closed the place up as much as he was able he went through it again, this time turning on all the lights. Why having more lights on should make him feel any better he didn't know, but so it was.

That accomplished, he still didn't want to sit down, stand still, or close his eyes—he might hallucinate himself being grabbed up and tossed around again before he could get them open. After a few moments of dull mental vacuum there occurred to him the idea of calling one or two people he knew, bad-trip specialists, whose help he had enlisted in the past. Never before for himself, of course: he enjoyed watching people take drugs much more than he did taking them himself.

Could he keep his head on tight enough, talking on the phone, to keep the helpers from suspecting that this time he was the one who needed help? He had damn well better be able to. He wasn't at all sure what they would do once they learned that this time, for a change, he was the one climbing the walls.

At the first number he tried a woman answered, with the information that the man he wanted to talk with was out. Walworth left his number with her, asking that the man call him back, trying to sound as calm as possible. He punched out his second number, and the woman he wanted had just answered when there came the sound of the buzzer at the service door, back in the kitchen.

"Hang on a minute," he said into the mouthpiece, and set the receiver down and tiptoed in his socks back toward the kitchen. On the way he observed that the gun was still, or once more, in his hand. Maybe the gun wasn't real right now, either. But he held on to it anyway. Silently he put his eye to the see-through on the back door, choking back his fear. Nothing, but nothing, was going to surprise him this time.

Or so he thought until he looked.

Seventeen

A sudden pounding on the front door jerked Clarissa into wakefulness. She had dozed off on the sofa, as it seemed to her only a moment before, despite the television set playing on the other side of the room, the book in her lap that she had been trying to start to read, and even her own unsettled thoughts.

She was alone in the house. About an hour ago, before the early December darkness fell, her angina had come on again. Not bad enough, she thought, to warrant calling the doctor. But still her last nitroglycerin tablet had been needed to ease the pain; with so many other matters to distract her lately, she had neglected to replenish her supply. So Judy, bless her, had volunteered to get more, and had gone off in her little car. There was no trusting the drug store these days to deliver anything, particularly in weather like this.

The pounding on the door came again before

she had got herself up from the sofa, and was echoed by a chiming of the doorbell. Clarissa, straightening slowly, muttered something, belting up her robe. Her heart was beating faster with the surprise awakening, but for the moment at least there were no pains in her chest. That at least, she told herself, was something. She was now on the brink of real old age, no doubt about it, and shortly she was going to have to hire a companion, or else persuade Lenore and Andrew to try to make a go of it again with live-in servants. It wasn't fair to Judy to depend upon her so much for the care of an old woman . . .

Most likely the knocking at the door was that of Judy herself; the girl had uncharacteristically forgotten her key for once. In her slow progress toward the front hall, Clarissa paused to switch on some lights. A quarter to five, and the sun should not be down yet, but the day outside the windows was as dark as night, and there was a heavy snowfall in the air, a regular blizzard in fact. Andrew was probably going to be stuck in the city again tonight, for once not on account of business reasons.

She flicked the outside lights on before looking out through the small viewer built into the front door at eye level. Just outside stood a man that Clarissa had never seen before, a rather rough-looking individual in workman's clothing, heavy jacket and wool cap. He was big and heavy, dancing a little in the cold, rubbing one exposed, blue-stubbled cheek with the back of a work-gloved hand. In his other hand he bore a long, wood-shafted tool of some kind, resting the butt end of it on the ground like an operatic spear. The upper end had been wrapped in plastic and Clarissa could not make out what it was. Across the man's face the falling snow made a multiple streaking blur, like a white beard.

He's come to tell me of an accident. Judy has been hurt. That was the first thought that came into Clarissa's mind. Simultaneously she knew there was no logical basis for this sudden fear; it was one of those chronic, baseless ones that seemed to intensify as one got older. But her knowledge did not ease the sharpness of it much.

Pain twinged now in Clarissa's chest. Gripping her robe tightly about her with one hand, she turned the bolt back in the lock and opened the door a crack, leaving the heavy chain fastened at eye level.

Seen without the mild distortion of the viewer's lens, the man outside impressed her at once as bluff and hearty. He was really enormous, and his blue shadow of beard reminded Clarissa somehow of her husband's.

He smiled at her in reassurance. "Hi, missus." His voice was deep and she found it confidence-inspiring. "My truck's stuck out here on the highway. Okay if I come in and use your phone?"

"Oh." Relief that there had been no accident washed through Clarissa, fluttering the pain. She smiled back, squinting into the narrow blast of frigid air that came in through the open door. "Of course," she said, and reached to move the chain. "Come in."

The drug store Judy was bound for stood just across Sheridan Road from the Shores Motel, in a small shopping center that seemed to have sprung up as unplanned as a patch of weeds amid the elegance of wealthy suburban housing surrounding it to north, west and south. As usual for the time of day, northbound traffic on Sheridan was heavy, and the southbound, Judy's lane, was light as she turned off the highway into the shopping center's parking lot. The snow was very thick, but it had not yet completely reconquered even the edges of the road since the last fall had been plowed away. A lot of places would probably have closed down early today, so that people could get started for home. Daddy wouldn't have started home early, though; he never did.

Getting out of her car, Judy squinted through driving snow toward the bright lights of the motel across the road. She wondered if Dr. Corday's room had been in the back or the front, upstairs or down. She had never even known its number.

Last night in her bedroom he had warned her, not to be careful, but to be brave. The police now seemed to think that the danger to the family was over, and they had withdrawn their listening post. But he hadn't talked like that at all. Anyway, Gran needed the medicine, and who else was going to get it for her?

The man ahead of Judy was buying cigarettes. Another woman was already waiting for a prescription to be filled. When Judy had handed in her scribbled paper, and it was her turn to wait, she wandered back to the front window. There she looked past magazine racks and jugs of colored water, through steamed glass that made the motel lights gigantic blurs.

A though that had been coming and going in her mind all day returned now with sudden force.

What if he came to her room again tonight? He
might very well. They certainly had plenty of
things in common, problems at least, that they
needed to talk about.

He was old, very old, she had no doubt of that.
But his age had a different quality than that of any
oldster Judy had ever met. It carried no weakness.
Was he older than Granny Clare or not? The question seemed meaningless, like asking whether
Chinese jade was more important than baseball. It
was unimaginable that he should ever have to
send someone out for a prescription.

Next to the drug store was a specialty dress
shop with a wedding gown in its front window.
On her way back to her car with Gran's medicine
in her pocket, Judy saw this, and the thought of
buying a long white nightgown crossed her mind.
Her sleepwear now was all girls' things, teen-aged
cuteness, plaids and animal designs. It was time
for—something different.

As she unlocked her car door, the electric signs
across the highway glared an intense loneliness at
her through the blizzard. Where was he now, this
moment? For just a moment she thought she was
about to discover him waiting for her inside the
car.

She didn't realize just how bad visibility had
become until she got behind the wheel and tried
the headlights, and found they didn't help very
much. It took skill and a measure of luck to pull
out of the parking lot and cross the southbound
two lanes into northbound traffic, slow though all
the traffic had now become. Snowdrifts seemed to
be growing up right under the wheels; most of the
pavement had completely disappeared.

It was odd, she thought, but the storm itself gave her no concern for him. From the first she had made it a habit not to think much about his strangenesses. But even without thinking she understood that his dangers and most of his problems were not the same ones that ordinary mortals had to contend with on most days of their lives.

Being herself a member of a family of ordinary mortals, Judy was still concerned to find out what she could about the storm and its effects, and turned on the car radio. "The Little Drummer Boy" was playing. She changed stations, to a jock babbling about a repeat of the great Chicago blizzard of '67. He managed to make it sound, as he managed to make everything in his world sound, like a prospect of nothing but infinite fun. But he conveyed no solid information.

For a little while she forgot the radio, having to concentrate on steering and adjusting speed so as not to ram the red tail lights just ahead. The highway, when she could see it at all through the blinded air, did not look at all like the same thoroughfare she had traversed only a few minutes ago coming south. Here a drift, though still a shallow one, had established itself all the way across, resisting the continuous work of wheels to cut a sideways segment of it into slush. At this point Judy passed her first genuinely stalled car of the night, which blocked part of what was rapidly becoming a single northbound traffic lane. She eased around it and kept going, at about ten miles per hour. Now she could once more spare a hand to switch the radio.

After three more tries she found a station giving some substantive weather information. Travelers'

advisories had been changed to warnings . . .
twelve or more inches expected tonight and tomorrow . . . wind from the east, the lake effect
. . . again, the great blizzard of '67. Judy's memory held one vivid record of that event, a picture of
a shoveled walk with walls of snow almost like
those of a tunnel on either side, their tops level
with her childish head.

As long as she could keep her car going at all, it
didn't seem that maintaining a more or less steady
five-to-fifteen miles per hour was going to be a
problem. The lights ahead were not trying to go
any faster than that, and those in her rearview
mirror held their distance cautiously. She
counted a few more stalled cars and then stopped
counting. They were already everywhere, sometimes up to their fenders in drifts, angled onto the
shoulder of the road, or, in one case, right athwart
an intersection and surrounded by futile pushing
men. Yet still the single northbound lane kept
moving, winding right and left among the fallen.

Daddy would certainly be spending the night in
town . . . he did that fairly often, usually, of
course, because of business . . . and Mother
would be stuck in Evanston tonight, Judy supposed, camping at some friend's house if she
could reach one, at worst settling into a chair in
the hospital lobby. They would be phoning home
by now, most likely, giving explanations.

Luckily she reached the next intersection on a
green light, so she was able to creep through
without stopping. Once stopped in this, anyone
without four-wheel drive might very well not get
moving again. Now only half a mile more. Things
wouldn't be *too* bad now, even if she did get stuck.

She would simply tuck her pants into her boots and make it home on foot.

But minute after minute Judy's luck held and her skill prevailed. She reached the home driveway in falling snow so thick that she almost missed the familiar turnoff when it came. Then she spun the wheel, gunned the engine, and her car lurched into the untracked drifts of the drive. Snow caught and held it, with a great feeling of finality.

Let it stay stuck until spring; she was home. With a sigh of relief Judy turned off the engine, pocketed the keys, tightened her scarf, and got out into the blizzard.

Looking toward the house, she saw at once that the front porch light had been turned on; Gran must be up, and would of course be worried about her, about all the family scattered in the storm. Struggling toward the light, squinting at it into the teeth of the storm, Judy was halfway across the drifted lawn before it struck her that something must be wrong. To begin with, there were huge tracks in the snow just in front of the door, and more of them than she could possibly have left on her departure. Worse than the tracks, a line of interior light shone out now at the door's edge. Gran had a thing about drafts, about keeping the cold sealed out . . .

Hurrying forward, gasping in the frozen wind, Judy tried to tell herself that what she saw were only signs that her father or mother had somehow managed to get home after all. The fantastic disasters of recent days were making her see perils and imagine monsters everywhere . . . it didn't help at all that this scene reminded her inescapably of that other house she had so recently approached, walking alone through almost untracked snow.

She reached the door and hurried in, gasping with sheer animal relief at the cessation of cold and wind. Automatically she made sure at once that the door was snugly shut behind her.

"Gran?" In the quiet of the house Judy could hear the television still softly playing in the living room. "I'm back." In her own ears her voice sounded louder than it ought to have, yet still it went unanswered.

The door of the closet in the front hall was standing open now, though Judy thought she could remember closing it after getting out her jacket and boots for the trip to the drugstore. Without removing any of her outdoor gear she walked on into the living room. The sofa where Gran had been was empty now, the television played for no one.

Judy walked on into the formal dining room, and stopped. Granny Clare lay on the carpet at the far end. Her old-woman's legs were crossed, one arm pinned beneath her body and the other one outflung. It was a pose suggesting not a simple fall, but the come-to-rest position of a body that had been thrown. Even before she hurried closer and bent to look at the still face, Judy knew that her grandmother was dead.

Pulling from her jacket pocket the medicine that would not be needed now, Judy carefully set the small bottle in its paper bag on the dining room table. Then she moved dazedly for the extension phone that stood on a small table in the hall. Picking up the receiver, she realized that she had no clear idea of whom she ought to call first—and then realized that it did not matter, because the line was dead. Ice on the lines, the storm . . .

But the act of careful listening had discovered another sound, an unfamiliar one, in the still house. Judy went back to the living room—glancing involuntarily into the dining room again as she passed—but could not hear it there, even when she had switched the television off. Further exploration showed that it was coming from somewhere down the cross hall in the direction of the old wing.

At the entrance to that connecting hallway, Judy paused to listen. It was a scraping or a scratching, very soft. It fit into no niche at all in her memory. It got no louder, came no nearer. But neither did it go away. It was repetitious, but not quite rhythmical.

For the first time it dawned on Judy that whoever had attacked Granny Clare—she did not doubt for a moment that someone had—could still be in the house. Conceivably the intruder had missed hearing Judy's return. Therefore she could now flee out into the storm again, and try to get help at a neighbor's. Police could be called—if all the phones in the neighborhood weren't out. Police would come—whenever the blizzard let them.

But even as she thought with part of her mind about running out of the house, Judy had taken the first steps toward her father's study. She knew he kept a gun there in his desk . . . and now, from down the hallway, there came a new sound that stopped her dead in her tracks.

"Judy . . . " The voice was ghastly, barely

louder or more distinct than the scraping that had
preceded it. It brought to Judy's mind an image of
dried snakeskin, being drawn tautly over jagged
bone. But despite the horror of it, the terrible
change, she knew at once whose voice it was.

She ran toward it, flicking on a hallway light.
To rooms on her right and left the doors stood
open, and closet doors stood open inside the
rooms.

In the doorway to the room that housed the
pottery collection she stopped. Enormous ruin
was before her. Display cases and tables had been
overturned as though in some giants' struggle,
glass and pottery alike smashed into a million
pieces. Almost nothing seemed to have been left
intact. The great terracotta sarcophagus that had
stood in the middle of the room had been cast
down from its base, and then broken, pulverized,
as by madmen with sledgehammers. The lid of it
was still almost intact, but it lay on its edge now
yards away, beneath a window where one small
pane was broken out. In through the hole a tor-
tured tendril of the snowstorm groped, a dancing
ghost in the near-darkness.

"Judy . . ."

She touched the light switch near the door.
Destruction sprang out at her in all its horrible
detail. A leather traveling bag, as unknown and
out of place as something in a dream, lay half open
in the middle of it all, and from the bag there
spilled a man's dark suit, clean shirts and ties.

Only after she took a step into the room did she
see him, lying in the middle of the one large open
space left on the floor.

Him? It was a scarecrow figure. It seemed to be hardly more than a suit of dark clothing that lay there, transfixed against the polished hardwood by a wooden shaft as thick as a hoe handle and a man's height long. This incredible spear had somehow been driven down into that floor, like a gigantic nail. Where the shaft of it entered the dark coat near the right shoulder, upwelling red was already congealing and drying into brownish jelly. And everywhere around the figure, the floor and walls and wrecked furniture were marked with red-brown gouts and splashes.

Of course the bloody clothing was not really empty, no more than that sheepskin coat had been. Dark cloth moved and swelled. What turned toward Judy was more skull than face, a loved face horribly transformed. Bared teeth grinned starkly white, the cheekbones bulged sharply beside a shrunken nose. But deep in the darkened caverns of the eyes, fierce life still burned.

Between those lipless teeth the snakeskin voice scratched out a question: "He . . . is . . . gone?"

Falling on her knees beside him, Judy spread helpless arms. "There's no one here but me. Gran's dead. Oh love, who did this to you? How did you get here?"

A dark sleeve tried to gesture. "Pull . . . out . . ."

"Are you sure?"

"Yes . . . I am not . . . as other men. Pull it out."

Straddling the shrunken scarecrow, Judy laid hands on the shaft. It felt unyielding, like something fixed to the floor as part of the solid house.

Hard as she pulled, it would not move. She bent to
get a better grip and tried again. Eyes shut, she
twisted and heaved with all her strength.

The old man made a sound that Judy inter-
preted as pain. But when she let go of the stake his
voice lashed up at her, more terrible for its very
weakness: "Pull!"

Eyes still closed, she straightened for a moment
and tried to pray, then gripped the wood again.
His fingers, whisper-feeble at first touch, came
creeping up the shaft to settle on it beside hers.
Now Judy threw her weight sideways, first this
way then that, like trying to loosen a nail before
you pulled it out. She felt the spasms of quivering
in the spear as his arms joined their efforts to her
own. She thought of wrenching at a nail with a
claw hammer . . . suddenly the stake pulled free,
with a cracking as of a barbed head breaking off,
down in the solid floor.

The abrupt release of strain sent Judy staggering back. She threw the horrible, broken-ended
thing away from her, and swiftly crouched at Corday's side again. Fresh blood, dark red, was well-
ing up now from the great wound between his
shoulder and his chest. His body shuddered, then
lay so still that for a moment Judy was sure that
she had killed him.

But once more feeble movement returned. "Better, better," rasped his voice, though it sounded as
lifeless as before. There was a pause. Then one of
his hands, its fingers hardly distinguishable from
bones, brushed feebly at the floor, re-creating the
sound that had first drawn Judy's attention to this
part of the house.

He said: "Bring here all you can of the dust . . .

earth of my homeland, you see. Fragments of my bed."

"Dust?" she wondered aloud. "Bed?" The only dust in sight was that from the crumbling fragments of the shattered sarcophagus. Obedient without really understanding, she began to scrape the pieces and their powder toward him with her hands. "So you rested . . . inside this," she murmured as she worked.

"He came upon me sleeping. Otherwise . . . but never mind. He will come back, or another even deadlier than he will come. So you must flee now, love. Run to some house nearby. Tell them to allow no strangers through their door tonight, no matter—"

"Here, I've got a bunch of this dust scraped into a pile. What do I do with it now?"

The sparks in his eye-caverns glittered at her thoughtfully. He said: "Push the dust under my body, along my side—no, do not try to lift me! I die quickly if you move me now. Else he would have taken me away with him—to her."

As though tucking a dry blanket beneath the fragile-feeling body, Judy performed the foolishness with the dust. As if playing a game that had to be won, however childish and ridiculous it seemed on its face.

She sat back. It was hard for her to look at his terrible face, his wasted form. She fought for control over her face and voice, and asked: "What now?"

His horrible voice said: "You must flee."

"I can run out somewhere, to one of the other houses here, and get them to call for the police. Then I'm coming back to be with you."

He shook his head feebly. "Police will be of no help to me. Any doctor they bring will order me moved. That must mean my death. Neither of us will be able to prevent it."

"Then I'm not leaving you at all," Judy decided. "What's the next thing I can do?"

"Oh, my dear," he whispered. And again: "My love." Then just when she thought her tears were going to break out at last, he ordered: "Gather more of the earth. Crumble the larger pieces to powder. You will find them brittle. It is the earth of my homeland, and very special to me. Mix the dust with my blood, and use it to stanch my wound."

Again Judy did as she had been bidden. She pulled back his ruined clothing to get at his parchment flesh, and fought to stem the flow of blood that still oozed richly from God knew where inside his mummified body. In all this nothing now struck her as horrible, except only the chance that she might fail.

At last the bleeding stopped. Judy had lost track of time, but her neck and back ached as if she had been crouching in the same position for hours. Her patient let out a sigh, and moved his whole body for the first time since she had found him, stretching out to what must be an easier position for him on the floor. Suddenly mindful of her first-aid training, Judy wanted to bring him a blanket, but he insisted that it would do no good. He also refused her offer to fetch an ordinary pillow, preferring that she slide a fragment of the broken sarcophagus underneath his head.

That done, he took her hand and pressed it in his twig-like fingers. "Thank you. Now, for the last time, Judy, again, I warn you—go."

"No."

"Listen to me. He who made your sister a vampire—yes, that is the truth—he will soon be back. I am still too weak to fight him, or even to get away."

She pushed back brown hair from her eyes. Her voice was hoarse. "I'll fight him, then. You'll tell me how."

"Oh. My dear love."

Her tears were threatening to brim again. "You do look stronger than you were. You can move, now, at least a little. Maybe if you rest a while . . . then I'll help you get away. Can I lift you now, and hold you?"

He nodded, feebly. Judy shifted her position, sitting on the hardwood floor. His head weighed almost nothing when she laid it in her lap. Gray hair and paper skin on bone. She stroked his forehead, too fleshless to have wrinkles. She told herself his face did actually look a little fuller now than when she had first found him. Though she had to admit that the improvement was pitifully small.

The deep sparks in his eyes burned up at her. "You will not leave," he said, stating a fact.

"No, I will not."

"Then you will be here when he comes."

"If he is coming. But yes, I'll be here till someone comes." With infinite tenderness she smoothed his hair.

His mouth emitted a ghost of its old hiss. "Then there is only one thing we can do. For your own sake as well as mine."

"What? Tell me."

"You know that I am not as other men."

"I know."

"Even wounded—so—it is possible for me to regain my full strength, or very nearly so, in no more than hours, or perhaps only minutes."

"Love, tell me how."

"The sun has set now and that helps me—of course it will help *them* also. Pulling out the spear and stanching the wound have helped me greatly. Yet one thing more is needed."

Judy raised her head. Had she heard a footstep, somewhere in the house? No, she thought, only the storm. Just inside the broken window, the narrow wraith of snowflakes danced and melted. "What is it, my love? Anything."

"My darling Judy, have I not told you again and again to go, to leave me here?"

"Stop wasting time and tell me—oh."

Her lover's hand had risen to the back of her neck, caressingly. First feebly now, then with strength surprising in a limb so thin, his arm urged her to bend lower over him.

Judy rearranged her own limbs, her body, to bend down in the way he seemed to want.

"Oh," she said again. His lips, that had appeared so dry and wasted, felt soft and warm upon her throat.

Eighteen

Before the immobilizing drug wore off, Carol bound Joe's arms and legs with strong cord and tape. She worked so cunningly that the bonds were almost comfortable, and yet when he was able to try to move again he soon discovered that he could barely twitch a muscle.

A preoccupied expert, Carol smiled at him absently as she worked. "Joe, my little dear, are you awake? Yes. Too bad, in a way. You might just have slept from here on. Don't worry, though. You're going to rather enjoy things at the end, I promise you that. It really does work that way. Now, all nicely packaged." She gave him a pat, then picked him up, dandling a baby effortlessly. "You must be packaged safely, because Mommy is going out for a while. I have to go and play with little Craig once more—to try to salvage him. Because at the moment he's the only breather I have left who'll work with me. And you breathers are so useful for some things. Yes, you are."

Carol carried Joe into an unfinished side-room, about eight feet by ten, hardly more than a large storage closet. Barrels and crates and boxes almost filled the place. A second door, the upper half of it glass-paneled, led to another, much larger, darkened room or area, where streetlight entering by distant windows showed bare concrete walls and floor, sawhorses, scraps of lumber, a can of paint or two.

He got only one glance out through the glass panel, for Carol promptly lowered him to the floor, left him sitting there leaning against something solid at his back.

Before she straightened up, she kissed his forehead briskly, as people who kissed their dogs might do. "I'd like to give you a real kiss, Joey, of a kind you've never had. But there just isn't time. Not right now."

Her feet in high heels tapped back into the finished rooms of the apartment. The door closed solidly behind her, so only the street lighting, very distant and indirect, reached him now. He could hear vague sounds of movement from the apartment for a little while, then there was silence.

They hadn't bothered to gag him, so it seemed he was free to yell for help as much as he liked—Johnny hadn't been gagged either. Well, maybe later he would try.

They hadn't even bothered to take away his gun.

The viewer built into Craig Walworth's back door showed him that Kate Southerland was standing just outside. She looked just about as she had when he had seen her last, blue jacket and all. Without consciously intending to do so, he spoke her name aloud.

His voice was low, but Kate evidently heard him through the door, for at once she rattled its handle.

"Craig?" Her voice coming through the thick wood sounded dazed and empty. "Craig? Let me in, please." Her image in the viewer appeared dazed too, staring glassily forward as if she could see him through the door.

Taking his eye from the viewer, Walworth turned himself around in a full circle, looking at his brightly lighted kitchen. He did not really see anything of the cheerful colors. His mind was devoid of plans, and he felt that he was waiting for something to be explained to him. When he had turned to face the door once more he tried looking through the viewer again. She was still there, and once more the handle of the door rattled.

"Hell, why not?" he said aloud. "Come in. If you're a phantom I won't be able to keep you out anyway, will I?"

It took him a full ten seconds to undo all the alarms and fastenings armoring the door, and then he swung it wide. Kate walked in at once. Before he did anything else he locked the door completely up again. Then he turned to look at her.

She certainly looked real and solid enough, and her confused state was even plainer than it had been through the viewer. Her face was paler than he remembered it, her hands kept rubbing each other nervously, her eyes jumped erratically about the kitchen, looking everywhere but straight at him.

Abruptly she began to speak in a staccato voice. "This place where I've been staying—you see, he broke in there today, while it was still daylight. Cloudy, but still so bright when I ran outside that I thought I was going to die."

"Huh." He studied Kate's face desperately, trying to make sure that it was real. If he fired his pistol at it, what would happen? "Somebody broke in on you somewhere, huh?"

"Enoch Winter." Her empty blue eyes flicked at Walworth, then past him at the stove. "He was looking for the old man, I know. He said—he said Joe had told him where the old man might be sleeping. He looked in all the vaults, I think."

"Joe," said Walworth, just to be saying something.

"Yes." Kate's eyes fixed on him suddenly. "Do you know where Joe is?"

"I don't know any Joe, lady," he said, suddenly remembering who Joe must be.

"I have the feeling that Joe has been here recently."

"Why in hell should Joe be here?"

"Joe shouldn't be in hell," Kate answered instantly—making as much sense, Walworth thought, as anything else that she had said so far. She appeared to stop to think. "I don't know why he should be in this place, then," she went on. "But he was here."

"My God." Walworth was speaking to himself again. "I think it really is Kate. Then there must have been someone who looked just like her in the morgue—someone they found in that rooming house—I don't know. God, what a day and evening this is turning out to be."

Kate nodded at him, a wise-old-woman sort of nod that made her look crazier than ever. "You speak of God a lot, don't you? They can, too, you know. It's not really like it is in the stories. They can handle holy things. They're no worse than we are, really."

"Sure, whatever you say." Suddenly Walworth remembered leaving the phone off its cradle, back in the other room. Immediately he felt pleased with himself for having his head on so straight now that he remembered that. "Excuse me one second," he said, and left the kitchen.

Sure enough, there was the loose phone; score one for the consistency of the world and the dependability of his brain. He hung it up, not bothering to find out if there was someone on the other end of the line now or not. He could call back later for help if it was necessary, but right now it looked like maybe he was going to fly home from this trip on his own.

On his way back to the kitchen he hoped fiercely that his visitor was still going to be there. She was, he saw with considerable relief, and she still looked like Kate. But a Kate still really out of it, staring now with great apparent interest at the icemaker on his refrigerator door—

Why couldn't he see her reflection in the chrome?

Some trick of angles—

Going up to the girl, Walworth quietly touched

her on the elbow, She started, not at all the way a phantom ought to behave, and turned her quietly wild gaze on him.

Those eyes of hers made him shaky. "Kate, d'you know what? Everyone thinks you're dead. Hey, now, don't start flying around outside the window, or do anything silly like that, hey?" He could hear the real pleading in his own voice, and it disgusted him.

She looked at him with a total lack of intelligence. "What?"

"I'm just telling you, don't do anything silly until I have the chance to show the world that you're still alive and in one piece. That's going to get me off one hook, anyway. Now you really *are* here, right?" He squeezed her jacketed elbow. "Sure you are."

"I'm here. Of course I am."

"Great. What brings you to my place tonight, anyway? Not that I mind." His hand, falling back to his side, brushed the butt of the gun still stuck in his belt, and he wondered if it would be smarter now to put the weapon away. He decided to carry it with him a little longer, just in case . . . in case of what, he didn't exactly know.

"I must find Joe." Kate's fine forehead creased in puzzlement. "I went to his apartment tonight, right after sunset, but he's not there. He's been *here*, I can feel it."

She raised both hands to her head. "Oh, those people drugged me, that night when I was here . . . maybe you . . . but you're not one of them."

"No, no I'm not."

Kate let her hands drop to her sides, and her speech fell back into its earlier lifeless tone. "I think I left something here . . . I didn't have any money with me when I wanted to go shopping."

"Shopping. Sure." Walworth stared at her for a little while. "My God, they really dosed you good, didn't they? Well, welcome to the club. I knew they were giving you something good that night . . . how many days ago was that? Almost a week, I bet, and you're still wandering. I hope it's not the same thing they gave me. God."

She looked at him as if she were trying hard to understand.

"So, what do I do with you now, Katie? Just call up the cops, I suppose. No, my lawyer first. Then the cops. Tell 'em you're here. Say you just wandered in. I know you slightly."

He decided to take a look around the apartment first, because there were probably a few things he'd rather the cops didn't see. He had better put the gun away, to begin with—suddenly recalling something else, Walworth turned his back on Kate and walked out of the kitchen again. When he reached his bedroom, the little shot-to-splinters table was lying just as he remembered it, on its side against the wall, dusted with a little plaster from the cratered wall above.

So, the shooting incident had been real enough—except of course he must have been shooting at a drug-induced hallucination. Carol herself had doubtless been long gone before things started to get dangerous. Her idea in drugging him must have been that he would eliminate himself with his own crazed violence—an unreliable method, it would seem, of getting someone out of the way. And why should she want him out of the way anyhow? Maybe this was only her idea of fun. He himself, he knew, had some ideas on how to have a good time that would seem far out, to put it mildly, to most people. But Carol and her pal the ape-man must be completely crazy. . . .

He righted the little table. Still, there was no way that the damage wouldn't be noticed if anyone came into the bedroom. I was cleaning my gun this afternoon, officer, and it just . . . they must hear that pretty often. But still the gun had nothing to do with Kate, or with her brother's kidnapping. So that would be all right. What he had to do now was show the world that Kate Southerland was still alive. After that, there ought to be lawyers around sharp enough to demonstrate to the world that whatever had been happening to Kate lately was not Craig Walworth's fault.

But this time, when he got back to the cheerful kitchen, his chronic fear was realized. Kate was gone. No trace of her. And the back door was still locked and bolted from the inside.

Partial relief came with the realization that she must have wandered off somewhere, and still be in the apartment. He found his front door still chained up, too, when his hopeful search for Kate took him that far. He stood in the living room and called her name a few times, tentatively. He was completely certain that that image of Carol, with a hole shot in her dress but not the pink skin of her belly, had been a picture projected out of his own doped mind. That had to be. Tonight's Kate, though, had looked worn and almost sick, and despite that—or maybe because of it—she had been very real.

Of course Carol, now that he thought about it,

never looked all that real anyway. Beautiful, God yes, but . . .

So he went through the whole place once more, calling Kate's name softly, peering into closets as he went and even under the beds. Doing this made him feel no sillier than anything else he could think of doing.

Once the gun in his belt pinched his belly when he bent over to look under a bed, and he had a sudden almost overpowering impulse to draw it out and put the muzzle to his head and pull the trigger. Would death be a drug-delusion too, an unreal sleep? Was Kate really dead and was he sharing the ultimate bad trip with her? When people got up from the morgue and walked . . .

His doorchime sounded distantly. Someone at the front. The lobby desk should have called up—or had he missed hearing the intercom?

This time he didn't even bother looking through the viewer first. He just undid the fastenings of the door and opened up, ready to take whatever came.

It was Kate again, standing there dumbly, looking just as she had before.

"How do you do that?" Irritably he reached out and grabbed her by the solid, real jacket sleeve and pulled her into the apartment. "Now stay put, will you, and let me think? I got a head full of shit and I got to try to think. Baby, I've got to be sure you're real before I call the cops to try to show you off."

"He's coming after me," said Kate, in her dazed voice that assigned nothing any gradations of importance.

"He? Who?"

"I went downstairs just now, and there he was, coming along the walk. He wants me to go back with him. Give me orders, put me out of the way somewhere, that's what he wants. But I've got to keep looking for Joe—"

Reality was suddenly as unmistakable as an onrushing truck. "Winter's coming? Up here?"

"—and he won't let me go on looking."

It was quiet enough now that Walworth could hear one of the front elevators running.

He ought to show the world one Enoch Winter, dead, along with one Kate Southerland alive. Winter had forced his way in, trying to attack her. Tell that story, and then let the good lawyers guide him through.

Quickly he closed his front door again, leaving it unlocked. His last look out into the lobby showed him the mirror with its draping raincoat. Show business, he thought.

Waving Kate to stand back, he retreated just a few steps from the door and drew the gun and thumbed the hammer back very silently. He raised it in a two-handed aim, keeping his gaze squarely on the door.

"What are you doing?" Kate's voice was suddenly changed radically toward the normal, as if the sight of the drawn gun had acted as a tonic shock. "Craig!"

The doorbell chimed. Somehow, with the distraction from Kate, he had missed hearing the sounds of the elevator stopping and opening.

"Who?" he called out sharply. His hands, center-aiming at the door, were very steady.

"Winter," the deep voice answered.

"No," Kate whispered, somewhere behind him. "It isn't. Be careful, don't shoot."

"Come in," Walworth called, his trigger finger very slowly taking up slack. "It's unlocked."

The knob turned and the door swung in. Not Winter at all. Almost as tall, but lean. Under an open black topcoat, what looked like a new suit of expensive black. A somehow Christmasy red tie, a fine white shirt. Smiling, jaunty, vigorous, but obviously old.

The old man.

I see now that you would only laugh like an idiot if I tried to tell you his real name.

Walworth fired. Even though he knew, before the gun went off, exactly how much good the bullet was going to do him.

Nineteen

Kate saw the old man step in through the front door, and in the same instant she heard the pistol fire. Only with that shock did her mind grow fully clear. If the old man had really needed help, she would have been too late to help him. As it was, she sprang forward with a speed and strength that she had not known she possessed, reaching past Craig's shoulder to knock down his joined hands with the weapon still clasped in them. The force of the movement knocked Craig to his knees.

The old man smiled reassuringly at Kate. Then, calmly bending with his own fluid and unhurried speed, he caught Craig by the shirt front and lifted him erect again, letting the gun stay somewhere on the floor. Reaching back with his free hand, Corday pushed the door shut behind him. Then he gently questioned both of the people with him: "Where is Joe?"

"He's been here," said Kate. "He's not here now."

Craig said: "I'm not gonna take any heat to protect her. Go over to Enchantress Cosmetics. Ask for Carol."

"And what does Carol look like?" The question was in a tone of mild interest. Walworth's strong, young body was swaying, and he seemed to be trying without success to avoid the old man's eyes. The old man seemed to be keeping the young one propped up with one finger.

"Real good shape," Walworth muttered. "Sharp dresser. Young. Red hair—"

"Ah? And where is the place you mentioned?"

Walworth named an intersection. "About eight blocks from here, west and south. I gotta warn you about her. She's really got it in for you."

"Indeed."

"And for me too," Walworth added hastily. "She wants me dead. Just today she drugged me—bad, man, bad. You wouldn't believe the things I've seen. I thought you were a friend of hers just now, coming to finish me off. That's why I . . ."

"Kate has told me," the old man softly interrupted, "how and where she came to meet them. Johnny has spoken to me of a bearded man driving a car, who asked him for directions."

Walworth's hands that had aimed the gun so steadily were shaking now. He couldn't seem to find anything to say.

Kate could only think of one thing clearly. "Please," she broke in, talking to the old man. "I can help you now. I'm all right. Let's go find Joe. He's in real trouble."

Still holding Walworth almost tenderly with one thin hand, the old man turned thoughtful eyes to Kate. "Go to the location this man has just given us," he ordered. "I shall follow presently." When Kate hesitated, he repeated firmly: "Go."

Kate nodded, turned, and fled toward the kitchen. There was no sound of the back door being opened, but Walworth knew that she was gone.

He asked: "You gonna call in the cops on me?"

"No," the old man assured him gently.

"You're not really here anyway, are you?" Walworth asked him, shivering. "I could almost wish you were."

At the mausoleum the old man had shown Kate something of how to use her recently acquired powers. How the night change in her body would enable her to pass like smoke through locked and bolted doors. The kitchen door went past her like some vague and insubstantial curtain, but this time she had hardly thought about the process. As she started down the back stairs of the apartment building, all her mental energies were concentrated on the job of finding Joe.

The back stairs were concrete and steel, designed as an interior fire escape as well as a service passage. Not until Kate had descended past two landings did she come to a small window. At once she used her marvelous new agility to leap up upon its narrow inside sill. Once she had located the knife-edge crevice where reinforced glass met metal frame, the closed window was no obstacle to her passage.

In the passing she willed an alteration in the cells of her body, the fabric of her clothes, the very air that filled her lungs and all the spaces in her bones. Outside, her altered body was at one with the wind. Her altered senses blurred. A creature of the air now, and no more solid than the air, she sank through clouds of falling snowflakes. Like blowing snow she skimmed above rooftops, down and up and down again.

Propelling herself by her will, she moved south, and west.

Joe was near.

His danger was terrible, but at least the threat did not seem to be immediate. And fortunately he had not yet been greatly hurt. Kate's inner senses were keener now than before, but at the same time sight and hearing had grown blurred and dull and indirect with her physical body dispersed to hardly more than mist. She felt rather than saw the glowing streetlights and the bulking buildings of the city below, and anything dimmer or smaller could hardly be perceived at all. In order to reach Joe she was going to have to take on solid form again.

In theory, she knew, the forms of animals were available now for her to put on. But she had as yet tried nothing like that, and at the moment she had no mental energy or time to spare for experimentation. So when she came down with a crunch in rooftop snow, her shape was her own, as human as before. And as her senses grew keen again Kate was at once aware not only of the details of the buildings and the storm around her, but of two other forms that were passing as she had just passed in the air. They were the diffuse bodies of a man and a woman that Kate was almost sure she had never seen before.

Joe was very near, now, but not in the building

where Kate had come down. She moved to crouch
motionless beside a chimney, while the couple
she had just detected materialized in a slow de-
scent out of the beflaked air to another roof only
half a block away. The building they came down
on was no more than two or three stories high, of
concrete gray.

In the little storeroom there were a couple of
fifty-five-gallon steel drums, with clamped-on
lids. There were wooden crates and cardboard
boxes. It was too dark to see how any of them were
labeled. Joe thought that if he could get to his feet
he could make an effort to spill one or more of
these containers on the chance that they might
hold something helpful. A box of knives would
seem to be unlikely. Maybe glass to break, to try to
get an edge with which to cut his bonds—if he
could move his hands enough to pick up anything. Something to start a fire with, to attract
help? He hadn't yet reached the stage where burning himself to death looked like a desirable op-
tion.

But it didn't take long to convince himself that
trying to work free of the ropes without some kind
of tool was going to be futile. Maybe if they left
him here two days unwatched he'd manage it. But
by then he would have died of hypothermia, or
whatever they called it now. The storeroom
wasn't as cold as the outdoors tonight, but even
with his jacket still on he was no longer warm.

The ropes were fixed so he couldn't stand. He
might be able to spill boxes, though. If one of them
contained glass, and if the glass broke, that might

help—more likely, though, they would just be irritated by his noisiness and come in and twist one of his fingers off.

There was one box on the floor, about as high as a piano bench and as long as a piano, whose lid was slightly askew, so that it ought to be possible to see or maybe reach inside. A place to start, something to try. Crabbing his way along the cold concrete as best he could, almost silently, Joe got beside the large crate. Here his face was in reflected streetlight, while the interior of the box remained in heavy shadow; looking in, he could distinguish only vaguely mounded white, about halfway down.

He had to find something to cut his ropes with, the way people were always doing it in stories. Anything.

At one end, the whitish surface inside the box was marked with a dark ring a couple of inches across. Just above that were two glassy spots. . . .

He froze, even the cold-trembling in his limbs suspended for the moment, and in that moment he was afraid that he was going to faint. A dead woman lay there, her staring eyes hardly a foot beneath his own. A young woman dressed in white.

Jesus. Jesus. His back against another crate, Joe slid away from his discovery, trying to keep from blacking out. His arms and legs were throbbing, and at the same time trying to go numb. If he fainted now . . . they hadn't even taken away his gun . . . .

. . . there were two voices again, somewhere out in the apartment. Joe understood that he was coming out of some kind of blackout. Probably a brief one, for he hadn't frozen yet, or wet his pants either. Something else to think about . . .

A Chicago cop shouldn't pass out at the sight of one more dead woman. It made his enemies no worse than before, he'd known what they were like ever since Kate's body had been found. . . .

Oh, God.

But it wasn't Kate. Blondish hair, perhaps, but—

In a moment Joe had pushed himself back in position to peer again into the crate, or coffin. Of course it wasn't her, he would have known at first glance if it had been. He forced himself to gaze into the box, trying to make out details that he had earlier avoided. It wasn't Kate, even allowing for death's changes. This woman was smaller, sharper-featured. And something was wrong about her mouth.

Out in the apartment, the two people talking had moved closer to the storeroom door. "You simply left him there," Carol was saying now. Whoever had been left where, she wasn't sure whether she liked the idea of it or not.

"He woulda died," answered the rough voice of Leroy Poach, who had been hanged in Oklahoma in 1934. "No way he would've lasted if I'd tried to bring him here. As it is he's prob'ly finished by now. I think I got him right through one lung. You shoulda seen the blood."

"Oh, I'd love to fly out there now . . . if I thought I could be there for the end." Carol's voice suddenly became a whisper of concentrated hate. "So much effort, so much time. Even you can't begin to realize . . . and now, to miss the end at last."

"Take off, then. Enjoy. I'll talk to the people till you get back. Explain to Lady Wanda when she gets up."

"No." Carol was regretfully decisive. "This conference is too important. I must be here for all of it, if I can. I must be unhurried, in control of everything. There must be no doubt in any of their minds that I am now in control. That the future is going to be what I say . . . Poach, what about the Southerland family?"

"They were all out somewhere, except the old woman. I put her out. It don't look to me like any of the others will get home tonight, the way it's snowing. If they do, well, they'll move the old bastard one way or the other, and that'll be it. Cops'll buzz around for a while, but the body'll be gone to nothing before they get a good look at it."

"Tell me again about the fight. I want to hear it all."

"Well. I looked in all the closets and everywhere as I went through the house, see? Then I got to this room in back, and I knew right away. There it was, a big stone coffin like the one I found out in the cemetery."

"It must have been earthenware of some kind, to provide the home earth. Clever. We must remember that for future use ourselves. Go on."

"Anyway, I just knocked it over and he rolled out on the floor. I got the stake in before he even got his eyes open. *That* opened his eyes for him! He managed to stand up, and we thrashed around a lot, but it wasn't really a fight. He didn't have a

chance—right through the chest. Nailed 'im there
like a bug."

When Carol spoke again her voice was low. "I
suppose it was for the best."

"Suppose?" Poach's voice did not really show
anger; rather it was as if he would have shown
anger if he dared. "In the two years since I met
you, you been drummin' it into me, how I gotta
kill him quick if I ever get the chance. How
dangerous he is. Also how much you hate him. So
I thought it worked out just perfect. I got 'im but I
didn't finish 'im. I give you the chance."

"Yes, you did the right thing. You have done
very well."

"You don't act too happy."

"Ah, dear Poach, don't sulk. It is just—can you
imagine what it is like, to hate someone for four
hundred years? You cannot, you are not yet a
century old. After such a length of time, there is
something like love in it."

"Love?" The tone was crude, incredulous.
What had been near-anger was near-laughter
now.

Carol's voice lashed at him. "Remember your
place, my man. What you were when I found you.
What you are and will be still depends on me."

Poach mumbled something.

"What?"

"Yes, my lady. I didn't mean. . . ."

"See that you don't."

The door to the storeroom opened without
warning, and Carol was looking in at him. She
was wearing a kind of green jumpsuit now, a
fancy party coverall, and she smiled at Joe en-

chantingly. Then her eyes moved beyond him, just as a faint noise came from that direction.

The dead woman had got out of her box and was standing beside it in her white gown, plainly visible in the brighter light from the apartment. She stretched luxuriously. There were traces of something dried around her lips, and she licked them with a perfectly pink tongue. . . .

. . . when he could hear the distant voices chattering again, and knew again where he was, he refrained for a long time from opening his eyes. He didn't want to see the walking dead. He thought about the sensations of numbness in his feet and hands. That he could assess them so carefully meant that he was awake now, didn't it? Before, he had been drugged. The woman in the box must have been only a drugged dream.

Joe opened his eyes, though, when he heard the door again. It was a smiling Leroy Poach, hanged in 1934, attired now in black evening dress, come to take Joe to the toilet. This prophylactic attention was actually just about in the nick of time.

"Wouldn't want you to be messy when we bring you out, cop." Poach was quite jovial now, despite his crusted forehead crease. It looked like a days-old wound, cared for and then forgotten. "Nice and clean and fresh is the idea. You're gonna be the piece de resis-*tahnce* at the party tonight. Know what I mean? Not yet you don't. Wouldn't believe me if I told you, either."

While being carried to the bathroom and back he could hear Carol and other people chatting, off somewhere in other rooms. He could see no one but Poach. The apartment was still mostly in darkness. There were lamps but no one had bothered to turn on more than a very few of them. Rusty water ran into the toilet when it was flushed, as if the fixture hadn't been used in a long time.

Back alone in his chill room, bound as securely as before, Joe thought he could hear more people arriving. There were more voices, and the voices were getting somewhat louder, as they tended to do at any party. And now Joe imagined that he could hear them talking Latin. At least he might have called it Latin, if he had been forced to take a guess.

Latin was bad, because it made him remember Johnny. Johnny in his closet, losing fingers. Then reporting the Latin conversations which nobody quite believed. . . .

Somewhere in the outer air, between Joe and the distant streetlight, moved something that was larger and thicker than a snowflake but just as silent as the snow. There was no way that he could see what it had been.

The box that the dead woman had climbed out of was completely open now, lid beside it on the floor. He had been hallucinating. If he looked into that box now, he would see something ordinary. But he wasn't going to try.

"But, why do we not speak English now?" said Carol's voice, not far outside the storeroom door. "Some of you in the past have chided me for using the old tongue too much. Poach, I think there are more guests on the roof, go up and ask them in."

"Thank you," said a man, not Poach. "English will certainly be more convenient for most of us. I suppose half of us at least have been born on this side of the Atlantic."

"And many of the rest," a woman put in, "have been here a hundred years or more. Long enough to forget a great deal of the Old World." Other voices murmured polite agreement. There was a nervous little female laugh.

Poach was back, saying something. With him came a man and a woman, new arrivals, for various greetings were exchanged. When that was over, Carol talked. She had become a public speaker now, addressing a gathering.

"I trust you have all had a tolerable journey, weather notwithstanding. Let me assure everyone that this storm is perfectly natural, at least as far as I and Poach are concerned. Our whole energies have been directed elsewhere."

Someone commented: "It's a great night not to be a breather." It had the sound of a quoted proverb. Again there was a scattering of nervous laughter.

When this had died, the hostess resumed: "As you know, this meeting was originally called that I might solicit your support in a struggle for our freedom." She paused. "That, I say, was the *original* purpose."

Another pause. The room they were all gathered in was suddenly extremely quiet.

And the shadow in front of Joe's streetlight was back again. Its presence was continuous now, but it was not still—there was a shapeless outline, shifting with some kind of movement. It was only the snow. What else could it be?

Abruptly Carol's voice rang out: "Your support in that struggle is no longer necessary, for victory is ours. This afternoon our enemy overreached himself. He attempted to attack Poach in his earth." This last was delivered as an indictment, made with disgust, as of an offense that was not only criminal but represented some ultimate breach of decency. "That ancient, evil . . . I scarcely know what to call him. That tyrant had evidently been taking his own publicity too seriously. He overestimated his own powers, and underestimated those of Poach."

A few moments of silence intervened. Then Carol, in a harder voice, continued: "Surely no one here regrets this turn of events?"

Another woman eventually answered. "It is only that we are—surprised."

Someone else murmured a faint question.

"No, he is not yet dead," Carol replied. "But he is firmly in my hands, awaiting judgement."

A man's voice, stammering a little but with more boldness than any of the others had yet shown, asked: "And who is to sit in judgement on him then? Of what is he accused?"

"Of—what—accused?" Carol whispered back the question as if incapable of believing that it had been asked. "Of what? To begin the catalogue, of attempting to murder Poach—but I can't believe that you are really serious."

Another man's voice put in: "I am older than any here, I think, except yourself, lady. If judgement is to be rendered on a *nosferatu*, a tribunal of seven is called for by the law. At least five are necessary, if seven cannot be found who—"

Now Carol's young voice snapped like a whip. "I warn you, I warn you all, things are going to go hard on his secret sympathizers. His crimes are legion. Even the breathers' histories document them. Do you think he is milder now, less murderous, less oppressive, than he was in the fifteenth century?" She paused. "Some of you, I think, do not yet appreciate the positive aspects of today's victory. What it is going to mean in terms of freedom for all of us. No more are we to be a powerless minority on the face of the earth, always hunted and in hiding."

A woman replied tremulously: "I think—I think we will all come to understand it better, in time. Can you explain it to us more fully, Morgan?"

"If necessary." Carol's—or Morgan's—voice went on. "That foul old man has had some of you completely brainwashed for centuries. That must be changed. When I call him old you know I am not speaking of mere spins of the Earth. He has been selfish and unchanging in his thought, blind to all our needs. Insisting that all of us be fettered by what he calls his honor. Not to use the breathers who swarm about us, not to taste their blood unless they give consent. Not to remove those who give us offense or stand in our way. Not to enjoy the treasures of the earth, that by rights belong to us as superior beings . . . but today a new world has been born. All that is changed."

There was a little silence. The speaker's voice was bright and confident when it continued. "Have any of you any more questions? Yes, Dickon?"

The pause dragged on before one of the men's voices dared: "I was only . . . I still think it would be better if we . . . "

"Poach, it seems we have an agent of the old man's here among us. Place him—"

"No, Morgan! I did not mean to dispute your

authority in this. It's nothing to me, really. He—he whom you call the old man is nothing."

When Morgan spoke again, her voice had grown even more light and cheerful. "Then enough of business, I think, for the time being. Would any of you care for some refreshment?"

Maybe if a man had to, if there were nothing else, he could break ropes with his arms. Even if his arms were numb. If he really gave it *all*. . . .

Twenty

As soon as the couple that Kate had seen descending through the air were out of sight, she flew again. This time she landed on the roof of the building into which they had somehow vanished. There she crouched in woman-form again, straining all her senses to locate Joe.

She knew he was very near now, somewhere below her, somewhere inside. His presence felt strongest when she approached a certain window. When she hung her head and upper body downward from the edge of the roof this window let her see into a large, unfinished room or area of some kind in which workmen's tools and building materials lay scattered. Joe was still not visible. But, as Kate looked into this window, her attention gradually became centered on a door at the far side of the unfinished space. It was a plain door, with a glass upper panel, leading to some kind of small, dark room beyond. Gradually she understood that Joe was there.

The window she was looking through was barred with heavy metal-and-wood grillwork, and wired with electrical alarms. But these gave Kate no trouble. Once inside, she moved straight across the empty, unfinished space, solidifying her body again as she came to the glass-paneled door. Joe, doubled over and bound, lay on the floor inside it, amid a confusion of stored boxes. His eyes were closed and he was motionless. But she was certain he was not dead.

Wanting to keep her senses at maximum alertness if she could, Kate did not pass through the closed door but retained her solid form and gently tried its knob. It was not locked, and swung smoothly outward. She rushed in silently to Joe's side—

She willed to rush to him—

The threshold, or something in the air above it, caught her like an invisible, impalpable steel net. She could feel no solid barrier opposing her, yet she was unable to reach even a finger into the room.

Kate shifted forms. The solidity of her body gone, she tried again. The doorway was as impervious as before.

In woman-form again, she stood just outside the open doorway, biting her nails and trying to think. The old man had said something about this. The room that she was trying to enter was living quarters, part of someone's dwelling. He had said it would be impossible now for her to enter any such space uninvited. Listening to the old man, back in the mausoleum, she hadn't really understood or believed what he was trying to tell her. Now—

She must rouse Joe, get him to call to her, invite her in. But she could hear other voices now, including the voice of Poach, just beyond the storeroom's inner door. They would certainly hear her if she called to Joe.

Again and again she pressed her body, in alternate forms, against the barrier. But it was like a breather trying to go through a wall. She tried urgently to force her thoughts into Joe's mind. But his stupor was too deep.

If only the old man were here. But even he would not be able to drive his way in uninvited.

Six feet away from her, she could feel Joe's life gently ebbing.

There were tears on Kate's face. She would have sobbed or screamed, but those in the apartment must not hear her.

The old man had told her something else. That whatever powers any human being could seize beyond nature came from the will, not through diabolism or magic. That if the will were strong enough, very little in this world need be impossible. That if—

Kate closed her eyes. She stood on the threshold, leaning forward. But she was not pushing any longer. That had proven useless. This was something else.

Is this what it means to pray? she wondered briefly. And then she ceased to think at all about what she was trying to do, or what was happening to her. Her self was entirely forgotten. There was only Joe, and his need, and the help that had to reach him, somehow.

Prayer, or giving birth. Or could they sometimes be the same—

—and something, some agony, was over. Kate came to herself lying face down on the concrete floor. Air, cold and unaccustomed, was filling her lungs with repeated pain, and it took a great effort to manage this labored, almost sobbing breath in silence. The birth, some kind of birth, was over, and the thin cry floating in Kate's mind was not a baby's but her own, unvoiced. She saw that she was lying halfway across the threshold. She crawled forward, arms trembling with a sudden weakness, the weakness of the newborn. With fingers that suddenly seemed almost powerless she began to work to remove the cords holding Joe's hands. He was still alive. His breath and hers were mingling in the air.

She whispered his name. That, or the tugging at his arms, made his eyes open presently. His eyes saw her, and yet they did not see; his mind had not reacted to her presence yet.

In her new relative weakness she was not going to be able to carry or drag him very far. So he was going to have to walk, and perhaps climb, and so she was going to have to free his legs. His hands were now free at last; numbly he moved them in front of him, trying to get the fingers working.

"Kate?" His voice was weak, yet loud enough to present a danger.

"Shh! Yes, I'm here. It's going to be—"

"Kate?"

"Oh, love, be quiet!" She pinched his lips together with her fingers, then closed them with a kiss. And now the last bindings on his legs were coming loose. And now—

The inner door of the room swung open suddenly. Enoch Winter stood there in dark evening dress. The difference between his face as Kate now sat it and as it was in her memory lay less in the new scar on his forehead than in the dumfounded surprise with which he looked at her.

Kate leaped to her feet, but would not flee alone. Winter's loud voice burst out with some exclamation; in another moment his massive fist had somehow collected both of her wrists within its grip. Other people came flooding around, gabbling their astonishment. A young-looking, red-haired woman barked orders. Kate was dragged stumbling out of the storeroom, into luxurious though badly lighted living quarters. At the moment it seemed that the last of her strength had been used up. Joe, looking worse off than she, his wrists gripped in Poach's other hand, was pulled along staggering at her side.

Joe didn't really begin to come out of his faint or stupor or whatever the hell it was until he was already on his feet. At that point Poach had him, was drawing him along to what Joe thought must be some kind of final confrontation with his enemies. Joe understood at once that Kate was now with him again, and in a way it seemed quite natural that she was. They were both of them now dwelling in the domain of ultimate things, of life and death. The trivialities making up what was usually called ordinary life had all been left behind—by Kate some days ago, by Joe himself only during the last few hours. Now they were in the land of life and death together.

Together they were pushed up against the edge of the massive worktable, on whose top Joe had earlier been drugged and then bound. The bonds were gone now, and he could stand. His arms were still so numb that he could barely move them.

"Bring her closer to the light." That was Carol—no, Morgan was probably the right name, Joe remembered.

Now Morgan was inspecting Kate's face closely. "She's certainly breathing steadily enough," Morgan pronounced a moment later. "I really don't think she's faking it." A murmur went up from the people gathered in the circle of shadow just beyond the table's light. Now Morgan was pushing back Kate's upper lip, as if inspecting a horse, then tilting back her head to examine the smooth skin of her throat. "This is Kate Southerland?" she snapped at Poach.

"Yeah, sure." Poach blinked. "Hey, at least it's the one that Walworth introduced me to."

"You assured me that when you were through with her, she had been changed."

In the silence, all of them seemed to be watching Kate's breath, steaming faintly in the room's chill air. Joe's breath steamed too. But he noticed now that no one else's did, except for the briefest momentary puffs with speech.

Besides Joe and Kate and the woman called Morgan, there were about a dozen other people present. Looking at their shadowed faces now, Joe could see that they were divided about evenly between men and women. Judged by surface appearances, the gathering might have represented a cross-section of middle-class America. A couple of people were black, one Oriental. Most were dressed in clothing that might have been worn to the office, a few outfitted as for a casual party. One sturdy, young-looking couple wore denim jeans and jackets that had the look of real work clothes. One of the older-looking women, rather beefy, almost motherly, was already gazing at Joe when his glance fell on her. She gave him a sharp-toothed smile, and in the middle of it her tongue came out and licked her lips.

Before he could start to think about that, his attention was caught by the girl who stood next to the beefy woman. She had been dead in the box in the storeroom when Joe first saw her. A blond girl, thin and nervous, as well dressed—he saw now—as a fashion model. Her eyes were resting on Joe too, and she was smiling.

"I have heard of this, but never seen it before." The speaker was a gray-haired man, the oldest-looking of the group. "A girl, or a young man, changed unwillingly. Then a few days later a spontaneous relapse to the breathing state. What the breathers, I suppose, would call a spontaneous cure. It happens under intense emotional stress."

"I have seen it, Dickon," Morgan mused. "But only once before . . . this is a genuine reconversion, it would appear. Her blood will again be good to drink."

There was a silence, while each from his or her own viewpoint considered this. Looking past Morgan, who stood on the opposite side of the large table, Joe could see a vista of semi-darkened rooms and halls, ending at a large, draped window, through which some exterior light sent in a filtered glow. If he could tear free, run on his

half-numbed legs, leap, cry for help as he crashed
outside . . . on Morgan's left as Joe faced her, a
great fireplace held cheery embers. There was a
tang of aromatic woodsmoke in the air. Above the
fireplace was mounted a lone diagonal spear.

As if struck by a sudden thought, Morgan bent
across the table to look keenly at Kate once again.
"Did any send you here, child?" Then she appeared to think better of the question. "Never
mind. It does not matter."

"Who would have sent her?" asked the gray-
haired man, Dickon. He looked round at all of
them, then back at Morgan. "What did you
mean?"

Morgan returned his gaze through narrowed
eyes. "It was in my mind that there may be others
who still cling to the old man's faction. A remnant
who have not accepted the fact of his destruction."

"Destruction?" Kate's voice was as clear and
loud as it was unexpected by them all. "She's told
you that the old man's dead? She lies!"

Poach did something to Kate's arms behind her
back, so she cried out and bent forward over the
table. Joe tried to struggle; in a moment he was
face down on the table too.

"What does the girl mean?" asked Dickon in a
shaky voice, looking round at all of them again.

"Mean? To prolong her life, if she can manage
it," Morgan answered calmly. "What else?"

A woman spoke up now, with timid reluctance,
but speaking up to Morgan all the same. "Where is
your prisoner being held?"

"Very well! If you still doubt me. He is miles
from here, nailed like an insect to a specimen

board. If any of you still doubt that, I'll fly with you to show—"

"Dr. Corday!" Kate screamed out suddenly. "Come in and help us!"

As if by a magic blow Kate's outcry cut across all other voices, even Morgan's, and wiped them into silence. Looking round him, Joe could see that no one was moving. The pressure of the silence was such that it felt like a growing weight. The grip pinioning his arms, though, did not slacken.

Someone's voice began a Latin whisper. It seemed to have no purpose other than to relieve the silence.

Morgan was looking over Joe's shoulder. The faintest of smiles was on her lips and her adolescent eyes had an expression that he could not read. Never again, though, would he be able to think of her as young in any sense.

The whisper had trailed away. The stillness in the room was more intense and ominous than before.

Poach was perhaps the first to move, letting his grip on Joe's wrists slacken and fall away. Joe saw Kate raise her head. He followed her gaze, in the same direction to which other silent faces were turning now. All were looking down the long vista of the rooms.

At the end the drapes were now drawn back slightly from the window. And someone was standing there, a man's form outlined against an icy city night now cleared of falling snow. The form was motionless as some effigy of wax.

"I knew," Morgan murmured. "I think I knew it all along." Now moving slowly, unsurprised, she turned her back to Joe. She took two steps toward that distant apparition, and her voice rang out boldly: "Come in then, Vlad Tepes! I say it now of my own free will. Enter my house, and we will settle all that lies between us, here and now!"

Twenty-one

Silently, with deliberate strides, the distant figure was pacing toward them.

Poach moved then, with such quickness that for a moment his great bulk seemed an illusion. Before Joe could react, the giant had reached the fireplace, and in an instant the eight-foot wooden spear mounted above it had come down into his hands. Morgan meanwhile backed up slowly, until one hand extended behind her rested on the table's edge.

For a long moment no one else stirred. Then, with a broken cry, gray-haired Dickon broke out of the group and stumbled into the next room. There he threw himself at the feet of the one approaching, who halted rather than step on him.

"Master!" Dickon cried out. "Master, I have never betrayed you. I would not believe that you were dead."

"Stand up, fool." For Joe's eyes, the face of the

speaker was still in darkness. The voice, resonant and commanding, was like Corday's, and yet unlike. It went on: "This is the new world now, Dickon, have you not heard? Such sniveling ill becomes one who is ready to take his rightful place as member of the superior race of beings."

Dickon's collapse became total. With his face down on the thick carpet, his words fell into muffled howls. The man whose path he had blocked stepped round him, and continued his advance.

The fashion model was next to fall upon her knees. "Vlad Tepes," she choked out, "we did not know . . . we never believed that you were . . ."

"When have I ever asked for groveling?" the newcomer interrupted. "From any of you?" He took one more step, and Joe could see that he wore Corday's face—and yet he did not. Like the voice, the face had been transformed. He who was not the old man Joe had known—and yet was—took yet another step. He stopped there, in a position from which he could see Poach and Morgan both.

In Morgan's left hand, held behind her back as if for support against the table, there had somehow appeared a long knife. In the table lights it looked to Joe as if it had been fashioned blade and all from one piece of some dark and oily wood. Near the fireplace, Poach stood poised like a harpooner with his wooden spear. The bloody mark on his forehead was throbbing now, looking almost raw.

For the moment, the two breathing people in the room were being ignored by everyone else. Joe saw that Kate's eyes were fixed, calculatingly, on the knife in Morgan's hand; all right, let Kate do something about that. Joe's left hand moved out stealthily over the surface of the table in front of him. His fingers touched and picked up a stub of pencil. If only it were not too big around—

"Watch out!" he yelled, and heard Kate's voice ring out in chorus with his own.

Had their warning been needed, it would have come too late, for Morgan's swift strike had taken them both by surprise. The old man had been ready, though. He was out of the path of the knife-blow when it arrived, and with a whiplash of his arm he slapped Morgan staggering back. Joe saw him vanish then. Poach's lunge with the spear found only air.

An explosion of frightened voices filled the room. All around, solid bodies were going out like candle flames. There was a howling exodus in the air. Joe had drawn his gun at last, and now he got himself in front of Poach. The giant was looking past Joe, holding the spear ready, seeking for Corday. Joe slid the pencil stub eraser-first down the snub barrel of the .38, felt it check in place, rubber against chambered lead.

Poach's eyes widened, discovering something behind Joe. Keeping the spear for bigger game, Poach lifted a free hand to sweep the irritation of a mere armed policeman from his path.

The revolver blasted once, and Joe's mind registered that at least it had not blown up in his hand with a jammed barrel. The hammerblow of the wooden impact slammed Poach's head backward, one side of his forehead disappearing in a great smear of jellied blood. The spear fell from the giant's hands, and the roar he uttered drowned out other shouting voices.

Though staggered, Poach somehow kept his feet. A second later, one eye showing clear and

horrible in a face half masked in gore, he was
coming after Joe.

Joe stumbled backward. With eyes and mind
and hands he scrambled to locate some possible
weapon made of wood. The table was too big for
him to lift. He crawled beneath it, but a moment
later it was knocked away. Lights went smash. In
the deeper darkness, screaming and rushing
seemed to go on without end. Joe, on his back,
despairing of reaching useful wood, raised his
pistol toward the huge form that bent toward him
with hands outstretched to grab.

A different kind of rush went past him in the air,
as of a grazing blow. Something struck Poach
with disembodied but elemental power, lifting
him from his feet. Joe could feel the floor vibrate
when the big body struck the wall.

Automatically holstering his gun, Joe got to
hands and knees and crawled toward the fireplace. Sparks were visible there, and there were
streaks of luminosity in the air, screaming, fluttering gigantic shapes and shadows. One went right
up the chimney with a shriek. A panic, as of
whipped animals unable to break out of a pen,
filled the place like fog. Joe groped his way amid
crazy smashings, outcries, smells unlike anything
he had encountered in his life before. What was he
doing? Yes, looking for the spear. But he couldn't
find it.

Turning away from the fireplace, he saw Kate.
She was halfway across the room, trying to hold
on to Morgan.

Joe charged, in mid-stride grabbing up a
wooden chair.

He swung the chair with all his strength. It cut

through empty air as Morgan's figure disappeared.

The chair landed on the floor, as Kate almost fell into his arms. Both of them were swaying with exhaustion. The darkened apartment was quiet now. They were alone.

Joe gripped Kate, looked hard at her while she looked back. He started twice to try to speak.

"We'll talk later," Kate said at last.

He nodded. "Let's get out of here."

Now, with a moment in which to look for it clear-headedly, he found the spear without difficulty. Kate, thinking along with him, had already picked up Morgan's wooden knife from where it lay on the floor.

They went out the front door of the apartment, at the bottom of a carpeted stair going down beside the elevator. Joe led the way, spear ready. It was a simple door that opened to the sidewalk—

Or to where the sidewalk was supposed to be. Joe had to push the door hard to make it open, and at first the knee-deep snow that had blocked it from outside seemed to him only one more artifact of the evil nightmare from which he and Kate were trying to fight free.

The night air was clear, the snowfall stopped at last. A keen wind was busy drifting whiteness over buried streets, impassable to cars. The old man, standing where the curb should be with his hands in his topcoat pockets, was gazing over a half-buried auto toward the other side of the street. There, almost directly under a bright streetlamp, a pair of figures waited, looking back at him. Morgan in her torn party suit, her cloud of red hair blowing free, looked tiny beside the giant man in evening dress, with the half-ruined face.

The old man did not turn to look at Joe or Kate when they came out of the building behind him. But he said to them calmly: "They will not fly now, or change their form. My hand is on them." He raised his voice. "Morgan, you see that my allies have not deserted me. Where are yours?"

Whether in answer to him or not, the woman across the street tilted back her beautiful face to the invisible sky above the electric lights. Then from her throat there burst a long, keen, eerie cry. It echoed away among the dark and lifeless buildings, above the brilliant snow, and was followed by deep silence. Joe, listening, could not recall such quiet in the city at any time of day or night. Far away somewhere, diesels were laboring, doubtless either plowing snow or dragging emergency loads through it. Poach was listening too, turning his raised face this way and that. Already his fresh wound was healing. Both of Poach's eyes were open again, and the blood that covered one side of his forehead was congealed in the frigid air.

At last Morgan lowered her gaze again to the old man. She shrugged. "If you can gather them in, from the four winds, they will doubtless be your allies now—for as long as you seem to be winning. Much good may they do you. Cowards, one and all. Gods, is it long life itself that makes so many of us cowards?"

Corday said: "The one who stands beside you has not yet lived a century. Yet he was cowardly enough to attack me in my earth."

"Oh, now we are to have considerations of honor." Morgan shook her windblown hair. "But then with you it is always honor, is it not?" She waited a moment, then added quietly: "We are going to walk away now, Vlad. You have won."

The old man made no reply. Morgan looked at him a few seconds longer, then turned away and began to walk. Poach, after a last wary glance, followed. Trudging through the deep snow to the nearest streetcorner, Morgan looked weary as some laboring woman struggling to get home. She turned there, with difficulty heading east into the wind. Poach lurched along beside her.

The old man took his hands out of his pockets and with each hand motioned one of his companions forward. He still had not taken his eyes off his foe. He walked ahead of Joe and Kate, keeping the distance between himself and his enemies nearly constant. The deep snow made hard walking. Joe wondered how long he and Kate were going to be able to keep up. The going was a little easier when they got to where Morgan and Poach had broken trail.

After leading them east through untrodden drifts for half a block, Morgan stopped and turned under another streetlight. "Drive us into a corner," she called back, "and it will be at your own peril."

Corday had stopped also, and once more waited with hands in topcoat pockets. "Alas," he called back cheerfully, "to our greater peril if we do not."

"Yours, perhaps," Morgan answered. "I speak now to the others. "Joe? Kate? He is as cunning as the Evil One himself. Don't you understand that if he is the survivor, he must kill you at the end? You know too much about him now, for him to let you

live. Kate, he has already killed your grandmother
tonight."

"And you?" Kate called back. "Liar. What will
you do with us—refresh yourselves?"

"You do not matter to us, fools. We only meant
to frighten you—you will be left in peace for-
ever, but only if you turn around and go home
now."

"This is the way I'm going," Joe told her. He
took a step forward, his grip tightening on the
spear.

Morgan looked at them all again, one after
another, then once more turned and walked away.
Poach kept at her side, walking unsteadily. At
once the old man followed them, and Joe and Kate
kept pace. Presently, under a blaze of neon from
the windows of an otherwise lifeless tavern, Joe
noticed occasional red-brown drops spattering
the snow.

At the next cross street, Joe could see other
people struggling along on foot a block and a half
away—perhaps trying to get home, or to get away
from home, or to find a doctor or an open liquor
store. With sunrise the city, still crippled but
aroused, would begin to live again and painfully
try to move. Then how would the chase go?

Morgan turned north. Holy Name Cathedral
appeared ahead, slowly fell behind as they
walked past it. Would there be an early Mass this
morning? Involuntarily Joe glanced at Corday's
profile, then up at the stone cross. The old man's
attention was not distracted from his enemies. He
did not even appear to blink.

Suddenly the going was easy. They had come to
a long stretch of sidewalk blown almost clean of

snow. Joe and Kate moved up to walk closer at the old man's sides.

Joe said: "It goes back a long way, doesn't it? Between you and her."

"It does, Joe. But all things must end."

"I heard Poach saying something tonight . . . that he killed Granny Clare."

"He did." The old man paced on for several yards before he added: "Judy was at the house also. But she is going to be all right—if we win. Now we must concentrate on the hunt. Our enemies are still deadly dangerous. But dawn is not far off, and it will weaken them."

"And you too," said Kate.

"But not my brave allies." Corday turned a sudden grin to left and right, including both of them. Joe wished to himself that the old man's face hadn't looked something like a skull when he did that. Still it had more life in it by far than many faces that were fat with flesh.

Corday went on: "If I should be destroyed in sunlight, and they survive, still they will be weakened. And forced to remain in human form until night falls again. So if I fall, you must kill both of them today at any cost. But I have survived many such wintry northern mornings, and afternoons as well—ah, they turn east again."

The distant diesels, or another squadron of them, could be heard again, a trifle louder now. Among tall buildings Joe could not be sure from which direction the sound came. Nearer at hand another noise was growing rapidly; a helicopter's rotors beat the invisible sky. Only a set of red and green running lights were visible as the machine darted past almost directly overhead.

The streets through which Morgan led them were still empty of other people; superb lighting shone on untracked snow. Another block east, thought Joe, and they'd be on Michigan Boulevard. Joe wondered if Morgan had a goal in mind or was simply fleeing. "They're sticking close together," he commented.

"As long as they do," said the old man, "I have no wish to encounter them without your stout support. Though they are perhaps gaining a little on us now, I think they will run out of gas, as I believe the saying goes, before we do."

Joe tried to speed it up a little. Police officer needs assistance. It would be a busy day in Communications. All furloughs canceled. Sorry, captain, I just couldn't make it in, there were these vampires I had to hunt . . .

Kate appeared to be doing fine. She walked with the long wood knife swinging in her hand.

"Corday, I said some things about you before. I'm sorry. What do your friends call you, if it's any of my business?"

The old man shot him a glance. "Your apology is thankfully accepted. I am comfortable with the name you know me by."

"Good enough." Morgan had certainly called the old man something else, something that Joe could not now recall. Well, he certainly wasn't going to push the question. If any reason other than gratitude were needed, he could well believe that there had been a grain of truth in Morgan's warning.

They were now gaining slightly on the enemy.

"You are doing excellently," the old man complimented Joe. He turned to Kate. "And you."

"I feel fine," Kate answered. "I wonder a little myself at how good I feel."

"This fortunate reserve of strength is doubtless a residual benefit of your recent life as a, shall we say, non-breathing human. When the life of your attacker who walks ahead of us is ended, weakness may come upon you temporarily. But then it should be about time for all of us to rest, hey?"

"Is it certain that I'm going to—to stay—this way?"

"It has been my experience that miracles do not reverse themselves. You will remain a breather. As long as that is what you truly want."

The pursuit emerged abruptly from between buildings onto Michigan Boulevard, as wide as some city blocks were long. Joe had never counted its traffic lanes, but all of them were completely buried now. Here and there cars, trucks, buses were entombed too. There was as yet no sign of snowplow resurrection. On every lamppost were festoons promoting Christmas commerce. The Boulevard was kept free by law from projecting signs of any kind, and the lines of its varied buildings stretched dreamlike to right and left, framing a cathedral aisle of clear snow.

There came a raucous buzz from somewhere, on ground level, nearby, getting closer fast.

Joe was first to identify the sound, and the first to react. Spear ready, he floundered out into the deep snow near the middle of the boulevard, prepared to defend his position there. He called out for help, and Kate and the old man were right behind him.

The snowmobile snarled round a corner behind Joe, and turned speedily in his general direction.

Facing Poach and Morgan with his spear leveled,
he heard it pass a few yards behind him, going
north. Morgan snarled at Joe, but her chance of
intercepting and seizing a conveyance had been
blocked. There were two people on the vehicle,
and one called out something cheery on seeing
folk in evening dress out for an early morning
romp. The words were lost in the engine noise,
and shortly the engine itself was fading in the
distance.

After a long pause, Morgan turned silently toward the east side of the street, and once there
headed north. Poach kept with her, stumbling
more noticeably now. Joe wondered if he might be
faking greater injury than he felt.

Above the city's lights the sky was changing
subtly and at intersections Joe could see the sky to
the east, above the lake; there it was no longer
dark so much as blank. He looked at his wrist
watch, but what he saw conveyed no meaning to
his worn mind.

Stoplights blinked out an elaborate ritual, tim-
ing nothing.

"Do you think they'll go into a building?" Kate
suddenly wondered aloud.

The old man shrugged. "We could follow. They
do not really want to seek a general involvement
of the breathing world, any more than I do. That
would be ultimately bad for all of us. Our branch
of the human race has the habit and tradition of
settling its own affairs."

"I just thought," said Kate, "if they keep going
east much farther—"

"Yes?"

"They'll wind up out on the ice. On the lake.

That's considered very dangerous. When people do that the police sometimes bring out a helicopter and pick them up, right, Joe?"

"Ah."

"Fortunately," said Joe, puffing steam, "all the copters in the city are going to be very busy today doing other jobs."

And still Morgan led them north. Going north would also, in time, bring them to the curving shore. Ahead, the gray canyon of buildings in which they moved came to an abrupt end. There, at Oak Street, the Boulevard melded with the Outer Drive and with a delta of lesser arteries. There the park began, and the beach. And, inland, the rank of tall apartment buildings in one of which Craig Walworth lived. "It's just hit me," Joe announced. "They're trying to get to Walworth's place."

Corday nodded. "That seems quite probable."

"You won't be able to get in there to get at them. If I'm beginning to understand how these things work?"

"Your new understanding is in general correct, I think." The thin lips smiled faintly. "But I was asked into that apartment a few hours ago."

"Oh."

And now they were at Oak Street. The white-shrouded curve of the Drive, for once as silent as a country lane, stretched away to the north under the streetlamps and the altering sky, strewn with abandoned vehicles. The wind off the lake, now dying, had ridged the Drive with snowdrifts. But unlike the Boulevard it was already scrawled with rutted tracks where something had managed to crawl through. The sound of diesels was again a

little louder now, and Joe thought he could see a
yellow snow-mover laboring far to the north.

Morgan and Poach still headed north, now
crossing blank white that had been parkway. East
of them lay snow-covered beach, and then a fan-
tasy of ice. Beyond that, more than a hundred
yards away, the almost invincibly open water of
the lake was leadenly visible under the changing
eastern sky.

When she had gone another block north, Morgan came to an abrupt stop. She stood there
looked ahead and inland, to where apartment
buildings rose above barren trees. Joe realized that
Walworth's building had just come into full view.
One window of it, about twenty stories up, was
leaking interior light of a different tone than the
light from other windows near it. In a moment he
realized that the glass of that window must be
gone—those windows were not made for ordinary
opening. Looking at the ground below it now, Joe
could make out human figures, beaming flash-
lights at one another and on an object lying in the
snow. Some of the tiny figures were wearing caps
and jackets of police blue. A black face showed
between an orange ski cap and a brown civilian
coat. Joe had seen that cap before; at this distance
Charley Snider's features were unrecognizable,
but fortunately distance worked both ways. An
olive-drab halftrack with a red cross on its side,
something borrowed from the armory, stood by
with its headlights helping to illuminate the
scene.

Morgan and Poach were standing still in conference. Now the giant raised an arm to point
eastward at the approaching dawn. The desert of

water and ice in that direction was becoming gradually more visible. The pale, still sunless sky above it was generally clear. Now the two turned and walked in that direction, not looking back.

At once the old man moved to follow, almost at a trot. Joe and Kate were gasping with the effort of staying at his heels. Joe floundered across a snow fence, only the top two inches of its ineffectual slats showing above curved powder.

Beyond the snow fence, forty yards of unbroken white ended in a jumble of foot-thick ice slabs, broken up and cast ashore by yesterday's or last night's powerful east winds. As Joe drew near the wilderness of ice its jagged horizon reached higher than his head. Above the ice beautiful streaks of pink were being born in the southeast sky.

First Morgan and then Poach vanished, this time in something like a normal human way, climbing into the cold maze of broken ice. Corday paused for an instant in his pursuit to ask: "Will it be possible for them to find a boat of any kind?"

"Not here. Not in the winter." Legs laboring, lungs pumping on frozen air, Joe labored after Corday's effortless, snow-plowing sprint, holding his spear at the ready, like a slow pole-vaulter, thanking God he had at least found gloves in his jacket pockets.

Following Corday's gestures, his allies spread out to his left and right, then followed his advance into the ice field. Joe had the worst of it, handicapped with the spear when two hands as well as two feet seemed hardly enough for clambering among the jumbled, slippery slabs.

Trying to keep Corday's head at least intermittently in sight, Joe advanced as best he could. The sky was light enough now to let him see what he was doing, but still the going was very awkward and treacherous. Moving silently was impossible, at least for Joe.

In a minute or so the whole city behind him was out of sight. Here it was as silent as Alaska, except for the sounds of his own progress. And, somewhere that could not be very far away, a gentle lapping of water against ice or rock or sand.

Joe lost Corday for a little while. Then, dragging himself up into a saddle between two cakes, he was relieved to see the old man's head and shoulders against a third, still and silent as the ice he rested on. He's probably letting me draw the first attack, Joe suddenly realized. The clumsy, noisy one . . . well, if that's the way we have to do it, it still has to be done. He gripped his spear and went ahead.

In a moment he had slipped on impossible footing, skinning a knee painfully inside his trousers and wrenching an ankle, fortunately not hard enough to cut down on his mobility any further. Joe cursed silently and gripped his spear and went ahead. When he got close to the place where he had last seen Corday, the chuckle of water was much closer too. It sounded like it might be eating at the ice right beneath his feet. If a man were to fall into one of these deep, dark blue holes . . .

Here was where Corday had been. But the old man was gone now. He and Kate must be nearby, following, listening even as the enemy were to Joe's clumsy progress. On the other hand he could imagine the whole chase gradually progressing away from him, and he, the dull-sensed one, falling and freeze-drowning here and never knowing its result. Someone would find him in the spring . . .

Ahead, around the corner of another tilted green-gray slab, an object of a different nature came into view. It took Joe a moment to recognize the tilt-topped mass of a concrete breakwater, draped as it was with smooth curves of ice. A few hours ago, great roaring breakers must have beaten on it. Deep water was nearby, then, underneath the ice-jam.

There was a small sound like a sigh, and from the top of an almost level lintel of ice at Joe's right the enormous form of Poach came leaping down at him from ambush. Joe got the spear around barely in time. The needle point of it made wooden contact, hooking Poach's dinner jacket and perhaps his ribs beneath. At the same moment, a woman screamed nearby and Corday shouted something.

The butt of the spear was jammed down against ice by Poach's weight on top. It rotated then, deflecting him in his leap to land with what ought to have been a deadly impact, on concrete sheathed in ice. A sound like a drumbeat was driven from his open mouth. The barbs of the spearpoint tore free. Poach slid from the breakwater into black open water just beneath.

For a moment he was gone. Then he surfaced at Joe's feet, mouth roaring water and air mixed, his eyes fixed on Joe. His huge hands scrabbled for a grip on ice or spear or enemy.

Groaning as if with his own death, Joe forced the barbed spear home once more. This time it went straight into the giant's throat. But Poach's long right arm shot forward. His hand locked on Joe's arm farthest forward on the spear shaft. They were going to go down together. Joe's feet were slipping on the ice.

Someone seized him from behind, just as he was being dragged to watery death. A thin arm round his waist supported him. He could not turn his head. A wave washed at Poach, and suddenly most of the exposed flesh of Poach's hands and face was gone. The next wave seemed to knock apart the bones of skull and fingers—Joe could hear them hissing, see them dissolving, as if the water were purest acid.

It was over. Even the clothing had gone down. The spear was bobbing in the water. Joe found his footing and shakily stood up straight. Turning, he met Kate's eyes. He started to ask: "Where's—"

Kate uttered a horrible little cry and struck at something on his arm. Poach's skeletal right hand dropped off, bones shattering when it hit the ice. The first direct rays of the sun were on the still-moving bones now. Joe watched them crumble into dust, and then to nothingness.

"Where's Corday, Kate?"

"This way. He sent me to help you."

Scrambling after Kate around a monolith of ice, he came upon the old man and Morgan in its shadow. The two of them looked almost like lovers seeking privacy. But Corday had the long wooden knife in one hand now, and his other hand held both of Morgan's wrists tightly behind her.

She was looking into the distant sky. Her eyes and face might have been carved from the slab she leaned against. Corday turned to the two breath-

ing people. "It is over. You may leave us now."
When they did not go he added: "What would you
have me do? Do you want to sentence her to one of
your prisons for her crimes? Leave us."

But when they had turned away he called:
"Wait. Tell—tell those who know me, that I shall
be all right. That I am going home."

Joe took Kate's arm. Suddenly she was leaning
against him weakly. It would be a struggle to get
back to where they could call for help, but they
would make it.

Behind them a woman screamed loudly, once.
That name, again.

Twenty-two

After the first preliminary session with Charley Snider and Franzen of the Glenlake force, Joe's head was spinning with exhaustion. But he still held to his determination not to collapse, and not to let Kate out of his sight, until she was ready to collapse too. As for Kate, she swore that she was holding out until she'd seen her little sister.

Snider obligingly drove them from Glenlake to the hospital, over freshly plowed thoroughfares. On the way he told them about Walworth's plunge through a broken window. Nobody knew yet whether it was suicide or not. But this time, the Homicide man made it plain, the authorities mean to get to the bottom of the whole business, once and for all—

Judy had been found at home, unconscious amid the ruins of the pottery collection. A pillow had been tucked neatly beneath her head and there were two blankets wrapped around her.

Someone had called police about her and fortunately they had been able to get a four-wheel-
drive vehicle to get her to the hospital. On regaining her senses, in a room near her brother's, Judy
had been unable to give any coherent account of
how she had come to be where she was found.
Examination disclosed that she had suffered a
moderately serious loss of blood. Internal bleeding of some kind was diagnosed, because no
wounds were visible that might account for the
loss. When the news came that her older sister
was after all alive, Judy accepted the happy shock
with no apparent surprise at all.

"Tell me once more now," Charley Snider
asked, going up on the short hospital elevator ride
with Joe and Kate. "Try to think. Where did you
two first run into each other last night?"

"I told you, I've been drugged." Kate looked
happily giddy. There was a Band-Aid on her arm
where blood samples had already been taken for
the police. "Somewhere on the Near North, I think
it was."

"I can't remember," Joe chimed in. "I can't
think very straight just now." He felt horrible, out
on his feet, and knew he must look the same, quite
bad enough to lend some credence to his story, or
lack thereof.

Snider gave him a look that said: We're going to
have a long talk soon. Right now Joe did not care
in the least.

"We got your grandmother dead," said Charley,
thinking aloud while he looked at Kate. "But so
far all the other Southerlands are still alive,
though some are damaged. We got Gruner dead.
And now we got Walworth dead, right out of the

building where Gruner was the doorman. This Corday is still missing. This Winter that you and Johnny describe is nowhere."

"Try finding Leroy Poach," said Joe, and giggled. The giggle had a strange sound.

"I think you better check in here yourself," Charley told him.

"No." Kate pressed his hand. "He's going to come home with me and sack out there."

"Thanks," said Joe. "I will."

The elevator stopped at Judy's floor and they got out. Two rooms down, the hall had police bodyguards.

"Daddy still glowers at you," Kate said. "He'll glower worse when I bring you back home. And then I'll punch him in the nose." Now first she and then Joe were laughing uncontrollably. Snider shook his head and walked off somewhere. A nurse came to stand looking at them doubtfully. When they had done their best to try to look like decent visitors, the nurse said: "You can go in now, if you're quiet. She's been asking and asking for you."

Snider reappeared from somewhere to follow them in silently. There was only one bed in the room, with a pale Judy lying in it. In a chair nearby Johnny sat in his bathrobe. Judy sat up with a jerk as they came in.

"We're all right," Kate got out. Johnny sprang up to give her his handless hug. She looked over his robed shoulder at Joe, appealing for some way to communicate the rest.

Joe tossed Judy a wink. "I have the feeling that the good guys are going to be all right now."

The pale girl couldn't help herself. "Dr. Corday too?"

Joe could feel eyes boring into the back of his neck. The ears of Homicide would be tuned in like dish antennas. What did he care? He was going to marry into quite a wad of money soon. "Him especially," Joe said, and winked again. "He can take care of himself. If I was him I'd be going back to Europe as soon as I could."

"The airports will be watched," Judy worried weakly.

"There are night flights, aren't there?" Kate commented. Let Homicide try to make something out of *that*. And Joe could hear Charley Snider's shoeleather creaking quietly out of the room.

"Oh, Kate," said pale Judy from her bed, "are you really all right now?"

"I think so. Listen, Jude. You and I are going to have a lot of things to compare notes on, when we get the chance."

"Oh, yes. Yes, we are."

"And then," said Kate, "I think we'd all benefit from a winter vacation somewhere."

"Great weather to go south," Joe put in.

Judy took thought. "Yes, going somewhere to rest up sounds like fun. Only . . ."

"What?"

"Maybe not south . . . they say the off-season is a great time to visit Europe." Judy's eyes had begun to glow, to dance a little. With one finger she picked at a spot, a tiny pimple maybe, on her throat.

THE END

FRED SABERHAGEN

- [ ] 55316-0   BERSERKER BASE (with Anderson, Bryant, Donaldson, Nivens, Willis and Zelazny)   (Trade) $6.95
- [ ] 55317-9   Canada $7.95

- [ ] 55320-9   THE BERSERKER WARS $2.95
- [ ] 55321-7   Canada $3.50

- [ ] 48568-9   A CENTURY OF PROGRESS $2.95

- [ ] 48539-5   COILS (with Roger Zelazny) $2.95

- [ ] 48564-6   THE EARTH DESCENDED $2.95

- [ ] 55298-9   THE FIRST BOOK OF SWORDS $2.95
- [ ] 55299-7   Canada $3.50

- [ ] 55305-5   THE SECOND BOOK OF SWORDS $2.95
- [ ] 55306-3   Canada $3.50

- [ ] 55307-1   THE THIRD BOOK OF SWORDS $2.95
- [ ] 55308-X   Canada $3.50

Buy them at your local bookstore or use this handy coupon:
Clip and mail this page with your order

TOR BOOKS—Reader Service Dept.
49 W. 24 Street, 9th Floor, New York, NY 10010

Please send me the book(s) I have checked above. I am enclosing
$_____ (please add $1.00 to cover postage and handling).
Send check or money order only—no cash or C.O.D.'s.

Mr./Mrs./Miss _____
Address _____
City _____ State/Zip _____
Please allow six weeks for delivery. Prices subject to change without
notice.

BESTSELLING BOOKS FROM TOR

MORE BESTSELLERS FROM TOR